THE MARQUESS MEETS HIS MATCH

JULIE COULTER BELLON

THE MARQUESS MEETS HIS MATCH

Lincoln Love Stories

Love's Broken Road

Love's Journey Home

Copyright © 2019 by Julie Coulter Bellon.

Published by Stone Hall Books

Cover Design by Steven Novak Illustrations

ISBN 13: 978-09997946-4-7

Printed in the United States of America

10 9 8 7 6 5 4 3 2 1

ACKNOWLEDGMENTS

I am so grateful to my family, friends, and fans who have waited so patiently for this book. It started out as a novella, but I quickly realized it needed to be a full novel. That took a lot longer to write than I imagined, but it kept me going when people would ask about it and be excited to read it. I hope it lives up to expectations!

I need to thank Jeni, Becky, Jodi, and Annette who were such a great support and read this book in several stages and through all kinds of changes. You guys are truly the best and I appreciate you more than I could ever say.

As always, my SWAT team is amazing and I am so grateful for all their help.

And my biggest thanks goes to my family who listen to my plot points, give suggestions, and always cheer me on. I love you!

CHAPTER 1

*L*ady Alice Huntingdon scanned the ballroom again as she moved through the steps of the quadrille, her gaze quickly flicking over the flower arrangements and ice sculptures her mother, the Duchess of Huntingdon, had ordered for the ball tonight. The white lilies and blush roses were beautiful and fragrant, contrasting with the kaleidoscope of ball gowns that swirled before her. Alice wasn't looking at the women, however. Her eyes searched the gentlemen who had assembled, needing to find Lord Pembroke. Had he arrived and not been announced? She was determined to have his name on her dance card for the supper dance. Then she'd be guaranteed to have some time to speak with him as he led her into supper.

Her current partner took her gloved hand as they came back together in the dance. "The weather is exceedingly fine tonight, don't you agree?" Lord Huntley squeezed her fingers, a hopeful smile on his face.

Alice sighed inwardly. She didn't want to give him any reason to think she'd welcome his attentions as a suitor. He had the right pedigree and was someone her father would ask her to consider if he made an offer, but she'd come to the conclusion that she wasn't suited for marriage. To anyone. "Why, yes, it is. The breeze from the terrace doors is quite refreshing."

She used the mention of the terrace doors as an excuse to discreetly glance around the room again just as Lord Pembroke was announced. He'd finally arrived. She let out a sigh of relief. He was the last person who had talked to Thomas Norwich, and she needed to know what their reportedly heated conversation had entailed. Thomas hadn't been seen alive again, and his body was pulled from the Thames this morning. She hadn't let herself think too hard on his murder yet. This was the first time someone she knew personally had been killed and, while her emotions were involved, she needed to stay professional. When she found his killer, then there would be time to remember him properly.

Unfortunately for her, her intelligence-gathering this evening had had limited results. She'd gotten all the details she could want about the latest *on-dit* that Lady Jane Wakefield had been betrothed to Viscount Farleigh. The viscount was old enough to be her father and had been married twice already. He had no heir, however, and was anxious to produce one. Sympathy had filled Alice at the news, but it was not the information she'd been looking for. Tonight, she needed to learn who had killed Thomas and why.

The dance ended and Alice smiled prettily at Lord Huntley. "A pleasure, my lord."

He patted her hand that she'd placed on his sleeve as they made their way back to her mother. "The pleasure is mine, my lady."

They made their way slowly through the throng of people to the edges of the ballroom, and Alice leaned into him just enough that their conversation wouldn't carry. "Did you hear the unfortunate news about the Earl of Moreland's third son? Some think he was accosted on his way home from his club early this morning."

Lord Huntley frowned. "I did. A terrible business." He tapped her on the nose, as if she were a girl fresh from the schoolroom.

"And not something for a lady's ears," he lightly admonished her. "Shall I fetch a lemonade for you?"

Alice gritted her teeth, but smiled up at him. "That would be lovely."

Once they reached her mother's side, Lord Huntley bowed over her hand. "I will return shortly with your refreshment."

Alice dipped her chin, watching him for a moment before turning to her mother. The duchess looked regal this evening in her turquoise gown and turban. The ensemble made her stand out in any crowd. "Mother, I—"

But her mother cut her off, tilting her head toward the impeccably dressed man beside her. "Lord Wolverton, while we are waiting for the duke to return, may I make known to you my daughter, Lady Alice Huntingdon."

Alice almost started with surprise, but held her reaction in. Lord Wolverton hadn't been seen at any society events since he'd been called home from war three months ago. His elder brother had been killed in a horseback riding accident, and his father, the Duke of Colborne, had suffered a severe apoplexy soon after. Lord Wolverton had been given the title of marquess, which his brother had held, but he would be the new Duke of Colborne when his father passed. He had understandably been in near seclusion since his return, but that fact had fanned the gossip.

Some said the new marquess was hideously scarred from the war and couldn't be seen in public. Others said he locked himself in his father's study and had been in a constant state of drunkenness since his return, barely able to stand. Obviously neither of those things was true. He was standing in front of her, presumably sober, since her mother had deemed him fit for introduction, and definitely wasn't hideously scarred, though there were two small white scars near his left ear and eyebrow. The edges looked ragged, and if Alice had to guess, they were from a small, dagger-like knife wound. Whoever had treated him, though, had known what they were doing. The scars were barely noticeable unless one was looking very close.

Alice quickly dropped her eyes and dipped into a low curtsy. "My lord."

When Lord Wolverton didn't respond, she rose with surprise. He was looking behind her, obviously distracted by something. A flush crept up her neck as her mother cleared her throat.

The sound snapped Lord Wolverton's gaze back to them. He hastily took Alice's gloved hand and kissed the back of it. "My lady," he murmured. When he straightened, he stole another quick glance around the room. Was he looking for someone in particular? Another lady, perhaps?

"Am I keeping you, Lord Wolverton?" Alice asked sweetly, barely able to hide her annoyance. She didn't have time to deal with an arrogant marquess. She needed to find Lord Pembroke and make sure his name was on her dance card.

Then Lord Wolverton's deep-blue eyes fixed on hers and for a moment she forgot why she was out of sorts with him. "Please excuse me, Lady Alice. I've behaved intolerably. Would you grant me this dance and allow me to make amends?"

His velvety voice stirred something deep within her, a prickly awareness stealing over her shoulders and down her spine. His eyes searched hers, as if he knew his effect on her. His lips curved slightly. Alice's pulse started to pound.

Her mother's sharp elbow in her side brought her back to the present, reminding her of his invitation. "I'd be delighted, my lord," she murmured. Placing her hand on his arm, she looked up at him, but he wasn't paying her or her mother the least bit of attention. His eyes were searching the crowd again. Who could he be looking for, and why did it matter so much?

They were nearing the dance floor when Wolverton's hand tightened over hers. "Lady Alice," he said, turning to look down at her. "Would you mind terribly if we took a turn about the terrace instead?"

He had an odd tone to his voice, with an anxious edge to it. Perhaps the person he was looking for was outside. If so, she would accompany him to the terrace, then happily leave him to his search and return to the ballroom to seek out Lord Pembroke. "Very well."

He practically pulled her through the terrace doors, as if in a great hurry. Alice walked as fast as she could without tripping over her skirts. What was going on? Lord Wolverton was acting very strangely. But all of that was forgotten when she spotted Lord Pembroke on the far side of the terrace. Now was her chance. She only needed to get rid of the man by her side.

"My lord," she said, breathlessly. "There is a bench just to our right. May I sit for a moment?"

He looked in the direction she'd indicated before he let out what sounded like a sigh of relief. "Yes, that's a brilliant idea." He led her to the bench where she sat down and arranged her skirts.

Out of the corner of her eye, Alice could see Lord Pembroke standing alone near the corner of the house. What was he doing? Was he waiting for someone? She needed to stay out on the terrace and see, which meant she had to think of something to talk about with Lord Wolverton.

"I miss the country where you can see the stars," she said, softly, raising her face to the darkened sky, careful to keep Pembroke in the periphery of her vision.

Wolverton was quiet for a moment. "When I was in Spain, the stars seemed so bright at night, as if someone had dropped a million diamonds on a black velvet cloak."

His words hung in the air, and she turned to him in surprise. The thread of pain in his voice was hard to miss. Did his memories of the war haunt him like they did so many others? "How long were you in Spain?"

He stared at her for a moment as if debating his answer, then turned toward the garden path. "Too long. Are you cold, my lady? Should we return to the ballroom?"

Alice glanced at where she'd last seen Pembroke, but in the moments she'd focused on Wolverton, he'd disappeared. *Drat.* "Yes, my mother will probably be looking for me," she agreed.

They'd just passed the hedges on the edge of the terrace when Pembroke appeared in front of them. "Wolverton," he said with a nod. "Lady Alice." He took her hand and bowed over it, giving her an appreciative smile and a wink. "A pleasure to see you again."

At the wink, Alice felt the muscles in Wolverton's arm stiffen, but he quickly relaxed. "Pembroke," he said. "I've been looking for you. Now that I'm back in London, I wanted to talk to you about going to Tattersall's. I find my stables don't have anything like the horses I had in Spain, and I'd like to see what England has to offer."

Pembroke barely spared Wolverton a glance. "Of course, of course. But first, Lady Alice, if you are not already spoken for, may I have the next dance?" He tilted his head and raised a brow as if daring her to accept.

Alice smiled. She couldn't have planned it any better. "I'd be delighted." She lifted her hand from Wolverton's arm. "Thank you for the turn on the terrace," she said as she stepped away from him.

But Wolverton moved in front of her, a fleeting scowl on his face before he was able to mask it. "Ah, well, for propriety's sake, Lady Alice should return to the ballroom with me, Pembroke. How would it look if she left with one gentleman and returned on another's arm? It could damage her reputation." He glanced at Alice and held out his arm to her before returning his gaze to Pembroke. "Once we're finished with our obligations in the ball-room, perhaps we can leave the debutantes and chaperones behind and have some real entertainment in the card room."

Alice nearly gasped at his audacity, implying she was merely a debutante and an obligation, but she pursed her lips to hold in any reaction. "This is to be the supper dance, Lord Wolverton, so I'm afraid Lord Pembroke will be quite busy with *obligations*." She gave him her best society smile.

"An obligation I will enjoy, I assure you." Pembroke stepped close enough that the toe of his shoe brushed the bottom of her skirt.

Wolverton swiftly captured her hand, and guided it through the crook of his elbow, holding it there. "Shall we go inside, Lady Alice?"

She kept her eyes on Pembroke, stifling her annoyance with Wolverton's high-handedness. "Yes. I wouldn't want to miss a moment of my dance with you, Lord Pembroke."

Lord Wolverton's fingers tightened over her hand and she could feel his eyes on her. She glanced up, and even in the low light his stormy blue eyes pinned her. "I'll be waiting for you just inside the doors," Pembroke said.

Hastily looking away from Wolverton, she fixed her gaze on Pembroke. "I shall join you momentarily," she promised.

Pembroke gave her one last glance before he went inside. If he was as taken with her as he seemed to be, he might give up the information she needed without a lot of prodding. *It might not be hard to get him to talk after all*, Alice mused. She quickened her step so she wouldn't be far behind, but Lord Wolverton held her back.

"In a hurry, my lady?" he said, arching his eyebrows and slowing his step.

"I wouldn't want to keep Lord Pembroke waiting," she said, nearly pulling him along with her.

But Wolverton stopped altogether. Since he still held her arm fast, she did, too, rather abruptly. Alice looked up in surprise.

"I must ask you a question, my lady. Why were you asking Huntley about the Earl of Moreland's son?" His voice was soft, as if she might spook if he spoke too loudly.

Alice gaped. How had he overheard? Swallowing, she forced

herself to relax. "I met Thomas once and was shocked at his death, that's all. There are so few details on what happened." She gave Wolverton a demure smile, hoping to cover her earlier reaction. "But Lord Huntley reminded me that such things aren't fit for the ears of a gently bred woman."

He tilted his head as if considering her words. "Since it was reported that Pembroke was the last person to see Thomas alive, is it reasonable to assume that is why you're so anxious to talk to him? To find out more details? If so, I'd like to know why." His blue eyes bored into hers. He wasn't going to give up easily, that much was clear, and she needed to claim her dance with Lord Pembroke.

Alice pulled her hand away from his arm and straightened her spine. "Lord Wolverton, this conversation has become tiresome, and I have promised this dance to another. If you will please escort me inside." She turned and started toward the ballroom doors, but Wolverton caught up easily and blocked her way.

His hands were behind his back now, the picture of a gentleman, but his voice was edged with tension. "Be careful, my lady. Curiosity can be a dangerous thing."

"Thank you for the advice," Alice said coldly. He held out his arm, as a gentleman should, but Alice didn't take it and moved past him. Before she reached the doors, however, a crack broke the silence of the night, and a brick shattered into fragments to her right. Alice found herself being thrown to the ground, with Lord Wolverton's body surrounding hers, cushioning the fall.

Alice lay on the terrace looking up at the sky she'd admired earlier, trying to regain her breath. Had someone just taken a shot at her?

Lord Wolverton's face hovered over hers as his eyes raked over her form. "Are you all right? Are you hit?"

She looked up at him, trying to gather her wits. "I'm fine." Her hip hurt, but other than that, she was unscathed. Pushing against his chest, she noted that he smelled of bergamot and mint.

Resisting the urge to press into his warmth to stave off the cold seeping from the terrace stones through her silk gown, she slowly moved to a sitting position, peering into the shadows. Was the gunman still there?

He stood and reached down to help her stand. "We should get you inside. Quickly now."

She barely heard him. A shadow was moving toward the back garden gate. "You're not getting away that easily," she murmured. Without a backward glance, she lifted the hem of her skirt and ran after him. The shadow must have heard her footsteps, because he began to run as well. Alice heard the clank of the back gate that led into the mews. If only she weren't wearing slippers!

She slowed and finally stopped just before the gate. It was too late. He was gone.

Wolverton appeared at her side, his breath coming fast. He took her elbow and pulled her around to face him. "Are you trying to get yourself killed? We need to get you inside. Now." He spoke as if she were a recalcitrant child escaping from her lessons.

"Go back inside, my lord," she said, her tone icy. "I know my way."

He stared down at her, his jaw clenched. "I can't leave you out here alone. You were nearly killed a moment ago."

"Not likely. He shot wide. It's a wonder he even hit the house," she scoffed. "*Nearly killed* is a bit of an exaggeration, don't you think?"

"No." He tugged her toward the house. "And I certainly never thought to be dodging bullets at a ball in London. We're going inside."

With one last look over her shoulder at the shadowy path that led to the mews, Alice allowed him to escort her back to the terrace. They walked in silence, his long strides shortened to keep pace with hers.

"You don't seem surprised," he said, staring at the terrace doors in front of them.

Alice glanced over at him. She probably owed him an explanation, but there wasn't one she was authorized to give. "I'm very surprised, actually." Surprised that someone had gotten through her father's security measures. Surprised that a gunman had been in the garden at all.

He gave her a brief nod before he opened the terrace door. "I'm glad you weren't hurt, Lady Alice. I'm sorry if I put you in any danger."

"Do you think the shot was meant for you, then?" Alice said, quietly, as she discreetly rubbed her now-throbbing hip. "Why would someone try to kill you?" She could be a target because of her work for the Falcon group. But why would anyone want Wolverton dead?

He lifted her hand to his lips and kissed her knuckles. "Ah, remember my advice about curiosity and questions, my lady."

She stared into his blue eyes, their depths serious and secretive. Who was he, really?

Before she could ask anything else, he released her hand. Once she was safely inside, he melted into the crowd surrounding the dance floor. Alice patted her hair and smoothed back the loose strands.

Someone had taken a shot tonight. But had it been meant for her as an agent, or Lord Wolverton, as he suspected?

She meant to find out. Immediately.

CHAPTER 2

*C*hristian stood on the fringes of the ballroom, arms folded, watching Lady Alice move into position across from the Earl of Pembroke. She was smiling and seemed poised, even though she'd been shot at mere minutes before. Any other woman would have gone into hysterics, but Lady Alice had not only taken it in stride, but had also run after the blackguard. Combined with trying to wheedle information out of Huntley earlier, she was plainly investigating Thomas's death. But who was she working for?

Christian moved closer to the dance floor, staying out of her line of sight. She was the epitome of an English miss with wheat-blonde hair and creamy, pale skin. But a thread of steel ran through her. Seeing her run toward a man who had taken a shot in her direction had made his blood run cold. What if she had given the gunman a second chance to shoot her? Christian had caught up to her, but it hadn't been easy. There was no doubt that if she hadn't been in ballroom slippers, she would have overtaken the gunman. What would she have done if she'd caught him? That thought was disconcerting.

Christian eyed Pembroke, who was looking at Lady Alice as if she were a dessert to devour. The sight sent a possessive jolt through him. Lady Alice wasn't his, however. He'd presented himself at this ball to provide an opportunity to speak with the Duke of Huntingdon, though finding him had been deuced hard, since he was the host. Christian's eyes roved over the ballroom once again. The duke wasn't anywhere to be found, but every other peer of the realm seemed to be in attendance. His gaze settled on Alice once more as she danced. Taking her to the garden in order to keep his eye on Pembroke had been an unforeseen mistake, but the fact that someone had taken a shot made his business with Alice's father even more urgent.

He loosened the neckcloth that felt too tight around his throat. It was strange to be back in English society. He'd been dedicated to the war effort—executing battle plans on the fields of Spain, then in France, cultivating contacts and strengthening the fragile peace they'd achieved after Waterloo. But when he'd received word that he was needed at home, Christian had sold his commission and returned to England. Doing so felt like leaving his life behind, in a way, since the army had been where he'd found his place in the world. But his family needed him, and that was enough. He was going to put all other matters to rest.

At least that had been his plan until one of his French contacts had gotten a message through with information that the duke needed to hear right away. By the time Christian had reached London and presented himself at Huntingdon House, the ball had already started. It was a crush and Christian had been searching in vain for the duke. Unable to sit idly by, he'd used the scant bit of information he had and tracked Lord Pembroke, but the moment he'd gotten close, shots had been fired.

He leaned against a pillar and watched Pembroke and Lady Alice moving across the dance floor. They really were an attractive couple, both blonde and the embodiment of everything noble and good about Britain. And yet, Christian didn't want her in Pembroke's arms. Or anywhere near the man, really, especially if he had participated in Thomas's death.

He straightened. The duke wasn't in the ballroom or the card room, but someone had to know where he was. He'd get some reinforcements, or at least a footman, to help him search and deliver a message that Christian was requesting an audience. The only problem was that the moment Christian's name had been announced at the ball, people had surrounded him, wanting an introduction or hoping he would dance with any of the debutantes in attendance tonight. He hadn't realized what a sensation it would be to see him out in society, and the attention was a nuisance. All he wanted was to find the duke.

Eyeing the doorway and his position in the ballroom, he hadn't much hope of escape without having to talk to anyone. Taking a deep breath, he came out from behind the tall, decorative potted plant. Several mothers with eligible daughters pointed at him with their fans, but he lengthened his stride before they could approach. He didn't have time for young ladies and their marriage-minded mamas tonight. Or anything else, beyond an audience with the duke.

The moment Christian gained the doors to the ballroom, he quickened his step down the long, portrait-filled corridor. His best bet would be to find the butler and inquire after the duke. There wasn't anything a butler didn't know about his household.

Turning a corner, he spied a smartly dressed butler standing nearby. Heading toward him, Christian nearly bowled over a gentleman who stepped in his way.

"Pardon me," the man said, then looked closer at Christian, his eyes widening in recognition. "Well, upon my word, if it's not Major Wolverton. You cannot be leaving so soon! The commander I knew would never have called a retreat." Edward Rutledge, Viscount Carlisle and a former lieutenant under Christian, held up his champagne flute, which was nearly empty, as if in a silent toast. "Had enough of this season's debutantes already, Major?"

Christian grinned at his old comrade-in-arms. They were nearly the same height with a similar build, but Edward's hair was nearly black, contrasting with Christian's dark blonde. The last time they'd seen each other was while celebrating the victory at Waterloo. Christian hadn't seen any of his men since he'd returned to England. "Well, at least I faced them instead of cowering in the foyer." He slapped Edward on the back. "How have you been?"

"Coming home has been an . . . adjustment," he said slowly, raising his glass in Christian's direction. "You seem to have done all right for yourself."

Christian stepped back and scrutinized Edward more closely. The smell of alcohol emanated from him, and though he was standing, he wasn't steady. The man was clearly foxed. "Edward, I—"

But Edward cut him off. "Come have a drink with me. We can reminisce about the good times we had together in Spain." He drained the rest of the drink in his hand. "Except that there weren't any good times in Spain." He stared down into his empty glass.

At first glance, Edward seemed well turned out, but Christian noted his mussed hair, the wrinkles in his cravat, and the haunted eyes of a man using liquor to mask pain. Though Christian had seen the same scenes of blood and death, chaos and destruction, a ball wasn't the place to have a conversation about the war's lasting effects. He jerked his thumb behind him toward the long corridor. "Maybe we could go outside and get some air."

Edward laughed softly without humor. "I'm not one of your women, Major. I don't need a turn in the garden." He pulled away, a little unsteady. "What I need is another drink."

Christian dipped his head. He wasn't responsible for Edward any longer, but he still felt a pull to call the man back, to try and help him deal with his demons somehow. Though he obviously didn't need a commanding officer anymore, Edward could use a friend. With a sigh, Christian followed Edward back into the ballroom.

"Wait," he called out, but Edward picked up his pace, headed for a footman holding more champagne glasses. Snatching one off of the tray, Edward turned to Christian with a grin and saluted him with the glass. "No more rules, Major. No limits on wine or women."

Christian took the last few steps and stood beside Edward and the footman. "Maybe there should be."

Edward took another long pull of his drink, nearly finishing it off. "We aren't readying for battle any longer, *my lord.*"

"And I'm grateful every day for that." He gave his former officer a side glance. "I'm here if you need someone to talk to."

"I'm fine." Edward gave the footman his nearly empty glass and took another drink from the tray. "I lived, didn't I? More than I can say for most everyone else we served with."

"Edward." Christian had so much he wanted to say, things he'd learned since coming back to England himself, but Pembroke was leading Lady Alice from the dance floor and heading straight toward them.

He stopped in front of Edward. "I'm surprised to see you here, Carlisle. When did you arrive in Town?" Pembroke said trying to hide his disdain, while eyeing the glass in the viscount's hand. "Lady Alice, may I make known to you Edward Rutledge, Viscount Carlisle."

Lady Alice curtsied prettily. "I'm pleased to know you, Viscount Carlisle."

Edward bowed and nearly toppled over, but caught himself. "I'm pleased to know you as well, my lady." He drained his champagne glass and looked around. "Your mother can count her ball a success, I'd wager."

"I agree." Lady Alice looked between the men and settled on Pembroke. "It's nearly time to go in to supper, my lord."

Edward raised his eyebrows at Pembroke. "May I steal your supper partner away for a moment, my lady? I have some pressing business to discuss that really can't wait, but I shall return him to you directly."

Christian narrowed his eyes. What business would Edward have with Pembroke? "Is there anything I can help with? I know I had unending estate business to attend to after I first arrived home," he asked cordially.

"It's nothing you can help with, Lord *Wolverton*." Edward smirked at him, drawing out Christian's title. "But perhaps I'll consider your offer in the future."

Lord Pembroke turned to Lady Alice, an apologetic grimace on his face. "I'm sorry to leave you alone even for a moment, but our business might take longer than is prudent to make you wait. I'll make it up to you, however. Perhaps at the house party?" His mouth quickly turned up in the same grin he'd given Alice earlier, the one that had been accompanied by a very forward wink.

Christian barely contained his frown. His gaze darted to Alice. What house party?

"Of course, my lord. I understand. Though your presence will be missed." She lowered her eyes demurely. "And I look forward to seeing you at Langdon Park."

"Are you sure I can't help you with something?" Christian asked, needing more information, especially if it concerned Lady Alice Huntingdon being in proximity to Lord Pembroke. "I am a man of many talents. I'd also like to renew our acquaintance, Edward."

Edward raised his eyebrows in Pembroke's direction and received an unmistakable shake of the head in return. "Thank you for your kind offer, my lord, but I'll have to decline. For now."

Christian dipped his head. "Of course. If you change your mind, I stand ready to help."

"I'll remember that. I think. But maybe not." Edward laughed at his own joke. "I'll have to write myself a note."

No one seemed to know what to say to his obvious inebriation and it was a relief when supper was announced. The crowd started to move toward the food, and Pembroke offered his arm to Alice. "I'll just escort the lady to her chair."

Christian and Edward bowed and watched them walk away.

"Pretty bit o' muslin," Edward said, wiping his mouth with his sleeve.

"Careful." Christian's hands clenched and unclenched. "She's a lady and as such, is owed respect."

Edward didn't even acknowledge that Christian had spoken. "Looks cozy with Pembroke."

Christian thought so, too. But was it an act on her part for information? He'd seen one or two female spies in France and Spain. Knowing the Duke of Huntingdon's position in the Falcon Group, he had to wonder: could his daughter be a spy? It seemed unlikely that the duke would put his only daughter in that position, but what other explanation was there?

He didn't have time to puzzle on it further. Finding the duke was his priority, but the woman walking away was quickly moving up on his list.

CHAPTER 3

*L*ady Alice was making polite conversation with her dinner partner, Lord Sutherland, silently cursing Viscount Carlisle for taking Pembroke away just when she had the chance to question him. Taking another spoonful of her turtle soup, she noticed a footman handing her father a folded note. He read it, his eyes traveling down the table to meet hers before he leaned over and whispered something to her mother and excused himself. Had he been informed of the incident with the gunman on the terrace? If so, she needed to report to him what had happened.

"If you'll excuse me for just a moment," she said to Lord Sutherland, who'd been seated to her right.

Lord Sutherland rose with her, holding his cloth napkin in his hand. "I hope all is well, my lady."

"Quite well, thank you. I'll return momentarily," she assured him. Hurrying away from the dining room, she walked quickly down the hall to her father's study. With a brief knock, she entered. "Papa, I saw you receive a note. I must tell you . . ."

Her voice trailed off when she realized her father was not

alone. Lord Wolverton's eyes fastened on hers, and she couldn't look away for a moment. He must have been a remarkable leader during the war, making his men think he could see into their souls.

Her father cleared his throat. "Lord Wolverton was just telling me how you chased a gunman in the garden this evening." His expression didn't change, the duke merely gave her a questioning glance. "Is that what you were coming to tell me?"

"That's not entirely what happened," she said, annoyed that Wolverton had gotten to her father first. "He shot in our general direction, and I wanted to know why. I was merely going to ask him a few questions."

Lord Wolverton snorted. "You make it sound as if you were about to invite him for afternoon tea. He *shot* at you. You could have received a second chance to end your life had you gotten any closer."

Alice shook her head. "He had a single-shot flintlock pistol, if I'm not mistaken. There wasn't any danger."

Wolverton took a step toward her. "He could have had another gun or an accomplice. Any number of things could have happened to you," he bit out. "It was reckless of you to go after him."

Alice pushed back the anger that rushed over her. She had to present a calm demeanor, as if he was merely discussing the weather. "I assure you, I did not require your assistance then or your opinion now." She moved toward her father's desk. "I don't take unnecessary risks."

Her father inclined his head, his shrewd eyes moving between her and Wolverton. "I'm sure with Thomas's death, everyone is a little on edge. And with the information Lord Wolverton has imparted to me this evening, I'm inclined to believe that tonight's incident may be connected to Thomas's murder."

Wolverton's jaw clenched, and he took a step forward. "Your Grace, that information is confidential."

"Yes, it is. Lady Alice has already been following leads and gathering information and she needs to hear what you've come to say." His gaze fell on his daughter. "Lady Alice, I'm sure you've been introduced to the Marquess of Wolverton, but we in the Falcon group know him as Wolf."

Wolf. For a moment she could only stare at the man. His reputation preceded him. Commander of men. Charmer of women. Legendary tracker. It was said he could find any quarry, even blindfolded on a moonless night. He was one of the most decorated agents in all of Britain. Alice had heard plenty of stories of his bravery and abilities to escape even the most slippery of situations. Impressed, but not wanting to show it, she merely dipped her head in acknowledgment.

Lord Wolverton stood very still, as if he couldn't process the duke's words. "Your daughter is part of the Falcon group?" he said slowly. "Your *only* daughter?"

"No one knows of her role, and with my own position kept under strict orders of secrecy, she's safe. And frankly, she's one of our best intelligence gatherers," the duke said without preamble. "Alice is especially talented with blades and getting information from those who are reluctant to talk. We need her skills."

"But if someone had reason to suspect her and put her name on that list, they could have been shooting at her." Christian looked at the duke. "We must look at every angle. Why did they choose your home for the attack and a time when your daughter was out in the garden? Could your identities have been compromised?"

"I suppose it's possible, but the number of people that know of my involvement can be counted on one hand." The duke sat down in the chair behind his desk and motioned for Christian and Alice to take the chairs opposite.

"Can someone explain to me what exactly is going on?" Alice asked, looking at her father. "How would our identities relate to Thomas's murder?"

"Wolf has received intelligence that a peer of the realm will be in Kent to exchange a list of names of British intelligence officers for a fat purse from the French. Thomas's death was merely to provide proof that the traitor knows each member of the Falcon Group from the lowest messenger to the highest peer."

"Your Grace." Christian looked her father in the eye. "As the head of Falcon Group and with a daughter who is involved, you and your family are in danger, I'd like to suggest retiring to your country home immediately, using several agents as footmen or stable hands to strengthen your security until we can apprehend the traitor."

"Yes, I agree, we should leave at once, but not so I can hide. Our country seat, Langdon Park, is in Kent, and we are planning our annual house party. This is the perfect opportunity to invite any nobleman who might have access to that list of agents and keep a close watch on them." He paused. "Our final ball of the party is always a masquerade. I can't help but think since the traitor is part of the nobility, he'll see that as a chance to stay anonymous while he sells that list and signs a death warrant for our agents."

"But will he dare risk committing treason in the house of a spymaster? He will know your position if he's read that list himself." Christian glanced at Alice. "And it also puts your family in close proximity to someone who isn't averse to killing."

"My family will be well protected, I assure you. If we remove to our country seat tomorrow, no one will question the timing as the house party is scheduled to begin a few days hence. That will give us time to strategize." The duke steepled his fingers and sighed. "When I helped a few French nobles escape the Terror, I never dreamed that it would turn into a double life of service to the Crown. But I don't regret it. And the few trusted men who know the names of those in service will be thoroughly investigated. A traitor among us is unacceptable. I'll do everything in my power to find them and their French buyer and make sure they are punished." His voice was hard, in a way Alice had never heard before, but it added emphasis to his words.

"Your Grace, the traitor likely knows that you and your daughter are on that list. Having a murderer in your household is quite risky and might not be the best course—" Lord Wolverton started to protest, but the duke stood and cut him off.

"There is much to do. For right now, however, if you would kindly escort my daughter back to the festivities, that would be most helpful. I'm sure her mother would appreciate her presence in helping with her hostess duties."

"Papa, I'd rather stay here and discuss the details." Alice gave him a speaking glance, but he didn't acknowledge it.

"I'll join you shortly." He came around the desk to kiss her cheek. "We'll have plenty of time to talk later, my dear. You and Wolf will need to compare what intelligence you've gathered already. Between the two of you, perhaps we can apprehend the traitor before the list is in play."

Alice's stomach sank. She didn't want to work with Lord Wolverton, but from the look on her father's face, he would not be dissuaded, so she capitulated. "Yes, Papa." Taking Christian's arm, she faced the door. "Thank you for your kind escort, my lord."

Christian opened the door and led her from the room. Many of the guests had already left the dining room and were filing into the ballroom, where the musicians were beginning to tune. Had they been gone so long? They must have. He stopped near the entry doors and turned to face her.

"It appears we're going to be working together," he said, keeping his voice low. "We'll have to learn to trust each other for a partnership to work."

She looked up at him, his gaze steady as he waited for her reply. He was in earnest, there was no doubt about that. "Yes, though I think that might be more difficult for one of us."

He'd seemed so shocked that she worked for the Falcon group.

Alice had met several men that didn't feel intelligence work was suitable for women. Was Lord Wolverton one of them? That was likely, but a small part of her was disappointed. Just once, she'd like to have a man see her contributions instead of focusing on her gender.

A few matrons stood on the far side of the dance floor, and Alice spotted her mother in the middle of the group. "Thank you for your escort. My mother is just there, so your obligation is fulfilled." And she was anxious to be rid of him. She needed to do a little more investigating on her own before she was saddled with Lord Wolverton as a partner.

Christian gently took her elbow. "Your father asked me to see you to your mother. I mean to do just that." He pulled her arm through his and slowly strolled across the room.

Alice forced a polite smile to her face. "As you wish, my lord."

When she finally reached her mother's side, she could see the anxiety in the duchess's eyes, which she was trying to hide. Alice touched her mother's arm and drew her slightly away from the group. "All is well, Mama," she said quietly. "Perhaps you should sit down? You look a little flushed."

"She's right, Your Grace. Allow me to fetch you a drink." Christian bowed slightly and strode away toward the refreshment table.

Alice watched him go for a moment, grateful that he wasn't hovering over her and was being helpful instead. Turning, she focused on her mother. "Father informed me that we're to go to Langdon Park tomorrow to get ready for the house party."

Her mother took out her fan and flipped it open. "If he thinks that's best. The extra time for preparation might be just the thing. Your father always invites a few more guests than I anticipate, but I can't begrudge him. He so rarely takes leisure time, and the hunting is good this year."

Christian returned just in time to hear the last part of her mother's statement. "My father once told me that the hunting at your country home is second to none, your Grace."

"My husband would agree." The duchess took the proffered drink from Christian. "I believe my husband is well-acquainted with your father. I was sorry to hear of the death of your brother and your father's ill health."

"Thank you." He coughed slightly into his hand. "After being away for so long overseas, I've been busy helping care for my father and see to estate affairs and haven't accepted as many invitations as I would have liked. Is it too late for me to accept for the house party?"

Alice started. Had he truly been invited already? And, if so, why hadn't she been informed?

"We'd be delighted to have you. I'm sure my husband would enjoy renewing his acquaintance with your family." The duchess snapped her fan closed. "Alice, I shall have to ask you to say my farewells to our guests, I'm afraid. I must excuse myself. There is much to do before we leave."

Christian bowed as the duchess swept past, her skirts swishing across the floor. Alice started to follow her, but stopped and turned to him. "For a man who is known for being mostly in seclusion, you have quite clearly stepped out of the convenience of that reputation by accepting the invitation to tonight's ball *and* to our house party."

"As your mother said, we will merely be renewing an old family acquaintance." He quirked an eyebrow. "And it would be hard to partner with you if we aren't in close proximity to each other. I admit, I'm looking forward to it."

Her heart skipped a beat at his low voice and daring glance. Did he mean he was looking forward to partnering with her, or to being at the house party? *Blast.* She needed to double her defenses when he was near. They seemed rather thin in his company. "Of course, my lord." She curtsied. "I will be happy to receive you there."

Christian stepped closer, a glint in his eye. "Why do I have the feeling that you are telling a polite falsehood, Lady Alice?"

She arched her brows and gave him her best society smile. "Because you are a very astute man." Turning to leave, she felt his eyes on her as she walked away, his quiet laugh following her across the ballroom.

Her grin widened at the sound, but she quickly sobered. With the news that the agents of the Falcon group were in very real danger, they had only a small window of time to find out who was giving their names to the country's enemies. If her father had a plan to capture the traitor at the house party, she would do all she could to help. Of course, Lord Wolverton being a partner in the investigation could make it infinitely more complicated.

But she was looking forward to the challenge.

CHAPTER 4

*C*hristian looked around the tavern as he lifted his tankard and took another drink. He fit right in with the rest of the men at the tables, with his patched wool trousers and battered hat. None of them had given him a second glance when he'd come in, and he'd been grateful to sit after a long day. He'd worked hard to put any thoughts of Lady Alice Huntingdon out of his mind by retracing Thomas Norwich's steps before he died. Nothing had seemed out of the ordinary, but he still thought that this investigation was too dangerous for the duke's daughter and was determined to be finished with it before the house party even started. Then the Falcon agents would be safe, including Alice.

He'd sent a discreet message to Nash, his best informant in Seven Dials, two days ago. Nash had finally sent his agreement and specified where to meet, but the delay in his response said he was more guarded than normal. Of course being seen in public was always risky for both of them, but Christian was always careful to take measures so that no one could connect them. Nash was late today, though. He should have been here a quarter of an hour ago, and Christian was starting to worry. He took another drink and resisted looking at the door. Where was he?

As if the thought had conjured him, Nash slid into the chair across the table, pulling off his dirty stocking cap. "Sorry, guv. Thought I was bein' followed." He stole another glance behind him. "Gots to make this quick."

Christian pushed the bowl of stew and a piece of bread he'd ordered toward his friend. "Have a few bites while we talk."

He watched Nash tear into the bread and hardly chew before swallowing. "There's lotsa talk about that toff who was fished out of the Thames."

"Anyone see anything?" Christian kept his voice low. Nash was part of a gang of mudlarks that scavenged the Thames, looking for anything valuable they could trade for coin. Not much happened at the river without them knowing.

Nash took two quick bites of stew and wiped his mouth with his sleeve. "He was wrapped in a fancy rug. Ewen jus' thought he'd found a rug and could clean it up and trade it for enough coin for a few meals. But the body was inside. Hadn't been dead long." He shivered and looked around again before leaning over the table and lowering his voice even further. "He said he saw a man in a carriage watching the riverbank, but when he saw Ewen, he drove away, quick-like."

Christian straightened. This was the first solid clue he'd gotten on the killer. "Would he recognize him if he saw the man again?"

"Don't rightly know. He's scared he'll be accused o' murder. Not talkin' much." Nash shoved the rest of the bread in his mouth. "All he said was that the man had light hair and a nose long enough to look down on anyone."

Which described half the *ton*, including Pembroke.. "I have a man who can draw likenesses of anyone. I'd like Ewen to help him draw one of the man he saw that night." Christian handed him another piece of bread, with a crown underneath it for the man's trouble.

Nash took both and shoved the coin into his pocket. "I'll tell him, but I ain't going to guarantee Ewen will do it." He surreptitiously glanced around the tavern. "And it's probably not safe to meet for a while. Somethin's afoot."

"Be careful. You know how to get information to me if you need to. I'll send a message about getting the likeness done."

Nash grunted before he stood, and Christian watched him hurry out of the tavern. Sitting back, he finished off his drink, making note of anyone who seemed interested in Nash or looked like they were planning to follow him. No one did. Perhaps Nash was being overly cautious, but when Nash had talked about being followed, the hairs on the back of Christian's neck had stood up. With the murder of a British spy, and a credible source reporting that others in intelligence were being betrayed, no one was safe.

When Christian finished eating, he paid for the meal and pulled his hat down low before heading out into the night. He kept his stride nice and even, though he was anxious to get home. Maybe it was Nash's words affecting him, but Christian's sixth sense told him he was being watched. On the corner, he passed two ladies of the night who called out to him, offering their services, but he waved them off. Holding the small pistol he had in his pocket at the ready, he didn't let out a breath until he'd made it to the edge of Seven Dials and hailed a hack. He kept up his guard until he'd arrived in Mayfair. Knocking on the roof, he let himself out and paid the jarvey, who barely gave him a second glance.

Reaching his townhouse, Christian went down to the servants' entrance and let himself in. He stole up the back stairs to his bedchamber, grateful most of the servants were in bed for the night and no one had seen him. After he closed and locked his bedchamber door behind him, he moved into his dressing room. It didn't take long to change out of his wool trousers and shirt, shoving the clothing in the very back of his wardrobe and donning his favorite blue banyan.

It had been a long day, and though Christian would have liked nothing more than to relax in front of his fire, he still had to meet with one more person. Edward had sent a note earlier that requested Christian find him at White's. After Edward's behavior at the Huntingdon ball, Christian wanted to keep that appointment. If he could help Edward adjust to life outside the army, he would. In fact, he'd been giving some thought to possibly establishing a trust for veterans. He wanted to do something for the men who had served; he just wasn't sure what would be most helpful. Perhaps he might bring the idea to Edward. If he was sober.

Christian pulled his banyan closed and belted it. Out in the field it had seemed easier to do what was necessary to complete the mission. Somehow, being home was harder. He couldn't explain why. Swiping his hand over his jaw, he squared his shoulders and rang for his valet. People were depending on him and he needed to keep moving forward.

Once he had washed and was dressed, he headed downstairs. His butler seemed to know his needs before he did and so his horse was ready and waiting. As he rode to White's, he passed several carriages on their way to evening entertainments. He hadn't missed the social whirl while he'd been away. Society's clamor for gossip and good matches had paled in the reality of war and stopping those who were hungry for power. Stopping Napoleon and those who stood beside him had been why he'd joined the Falcon Group. Their missions had made him believe they could win and they had. But now, someone was threatening the peace they'd achieved. His mind went over the scant clues they had on the traitor's identity. A British peer. Possibly blonde. A long nose. Christian let out a frustrated breath. It wasn't much.

Before long, he was striding into White's. Several patrons greeted him and invited him to sit at their table, but he politely declined. He really wasn't in the mood to socialize or talk about his father, his brother, the war, or anything else that members of the *ton* seemed eager to ask him. He wanted to find Edward as soon as possible.

After looking in several rooms, Christian finally gave up and stopped a passing footman. "Has Viscount Carlisle been here tonight?"

"Yes, my lord. He was drinking with Lord Pembroke earlier, and they left together an hour past." The servant dipped his head. "Is there anything else?"

"No, that is all." Christian let out a frustrated breath. Why would Edward call him here only to leave? And what could Pembroke and Edward have to talk about? Surely Edward wouldn't be party to any traitorous actions. He'd fought and sacrificed for England. But Christian had to admit that Edward hadn't seemed himself at the ball. Rubbing the back of his neck, he added Edward Carlisle's name to his growing list of peers who needed to be investigated as the possible traitor.

As he stalked to the entrance and waited for his horse, Christian couldn't stop thinking about Edward and the last battle they'd been in together. The unmistakable fear, combined with the raw courage of his men, haunted him the most. Seeing Edward struggling with those same demons brought out feelings he'd rather stay buried. Pushing his thoughts away, Christian mounted and took the reins, turning the horse's head and guiding him home. The darkness, combined with the nip in the air, reminded him of his last march in Spain. He'd been tired then, too, and trying to guide his horse through congested roads. But he was in England now, and he didn't have to worry about food, warmth, or if his men could survive one more battle.

More than once, he'd had to remind himself that the war was over.

He stopped in front of his townhouse and stared up at it. Stone steps led up to the three-story building that was so familiar to him. He had so many memories of joking with his father and brother here. This would always be considered their bachelor lodgings while Parliament was in session. Christian's mother had died in childbirth so it had just been the three of them. It wasn't until he was much older that he realized most fathers, especially dukes, didn't take an active role in the upbringing of their children. But his father had loved them and showed it. Christian's heart clenched anew that John was gone, and his father would soon be joining him.

Slowly climbing the steps, Christian nodded to the butler as he went inside and headed directly to his study. "I don't want to be disturbed, Carruthers," he said as he passed.

He needed a drink. Maybe two. He wanted to numb the grief, the war, everything. But with his fingertips on the door handle, he stopped. He'd made a promise after drinking himself into a stupor the first few weeks he'd returned home. He didn't have to drown in alcohol or in memories. He was stronger than that. Facing his demons was the solution, even if he did it one day at a time. Turning on his heel, he went directly to his bedchamber and closed the door.

Sitting down in the overstuffed chair, Christian took off his boots. Wiggling his toes, he stretched them out toward the fire and stared at the flames. If he looked long enough he'd be able to see the grim faces of his men that had surrounded a small but warm fire the night before they'd breached the walls of Badajoz. They'd lost so many soldiers that day— their screams as they died still echoed through his dreams. But he'd tried to make peace with their loss and his survival by working in intelligence and making sure their sacrifices hadn't been in vain. Edward would have to reach that point himself before he could attempt to move forward from the past. Hopefully his business with Pembroke wouldn't make anything worse—like being hanged for treason.

He closed his eyes for just a moment, needing to rest but not wanting to dream. His body finally succumbed to slumber, however, and this night, his dreams involved chasing Alice through a garden. She was laughing, and he wanted to reach her, to keep her close and safe next to him.

A distinctly male voice cut through his dream. "My lord."

Christian opened one eye. It was Brooks, his valet. "What's wrong?" Sitting up in the chair, Christian rubbed his sore neck muscles.

"I've brought you some breakfast, my lord." Brooks pointed to the tray on the table behind him. "You left instructions with me yesterday about getting an early start to Langdon Park this morning."

Christian nodded. Several agents were heading to Langdon Park today to tighten security for the duke. It was also the beginning of the Huntingdon house party and Christian wanted to be one of the first to arrive. He was looking forward to getting an update from the duke and seeing if Alice had gathered any more information. As partners, he planned to keep her busy with intelligence gathering and far away from anything dangerous.

After he'd breakfasted, Christian opened the daily update from his father's physician. The little flicker of hope in his heart burned a little brighter. Maybe this time the letter would say his father was getting well. But Christian's eyes scanned the parchment. There was no change. No matter how hard he hoped for different news, it was always the same. The duke was not expected to live.

His heart heavy, Christian finished taking care of some mundane estate matters, making sure to leave his direction for the physician and instructions to inform him immediately of any change with his father's condition. With the last details taken care of, he went out to his horse. After checking his saddlebags, he mounted and rode toward the outskirts of London. A long ride was just what he needed to clear his head. If the weather held and the roads were good, he would reach Langdon Park before nightfall.

Not wanting to dwell on his father's condition, Christian turned his thoughts to what his next move might be to stop the traitor. The first thing on the agenda was to ensure the safety of the duke and his family. One attempt had already been made on Alice's life; he was sure of it. Why else would a shot be taken at her while at home? Then he needed to discreetly question Lord Pembroke. He thought of his bold wink at Lady Alice on the terrace and was irritated all over again. Yes, until he determined Lord Pembroke's guilt or innocence, he would keep Alice's inter-action with Pembroke to a minimum. For safety's sake.

When he finally arrived at the country estate, it was nearly sunset. The two-story mansion was set on a small hill to show it off to its best advantage. The last rays of the sun made the stones look warm and inviting. Like many country estates, Langdon Park had been the country seat for the dukedom for hundreds of years, and the architecture was grand and meant to impress from the castellated roof and turrets to the oriel windows. The rolling lawn and trees surrounding the house were inviting, and a lake sparkled in the distance.

As Christian rode closer, a groom came out to greet him. "May I take your horse, my lord?" he asked, bowing and tugging his forelock.

"If I didn't know you as well as I do, Pearce, I wouldn't have ever guessed you haven't been in service all your life." Christian dismounted and grinned, barely holding back from hugging the man he'd served with and considered a brother. "I'm surprised to see you. I thought you were still in France."

"That's where I prefer everyone to think I am." Jack Pearce had been extremely useful behind enemy lines and had saved countless lives monitoring French movements and getting the information to those in charge. He was also one of the best snipers the British army had. "Wanted to be here for the duke, though. If my name's about to be sold, I'd like a hand in stopping that."

"The duke is lucky to have you." Christian gave his horse's flank a pat before Pearce took the reins.

Pearce grinned, giving him a bow. "It's good to be back together, playing our parts like the old days. You find 'em, and I finish 'em."

"Hopefully our luck holds out." Christian smiled and watched Pearce lead the horse to the stables. The man was a crack shot, and they'd worked well together in the field against the enemy. It was still shocking that their services were needed so close to home.

Christian brushed at his clothes as he approached the door of the house, trying to get some of the road's dust off before he saw the duke. Or Lady Alice.

The butler opened it wide and admitted Christian inside. "My lord, we've been expecting you," he intoned.

Before he could respond, the duchess spoke from the top of the stairs.

"Lord Wolverton, I'm pleased you've arrived," Lady Huntingdon said as she descended the grand staircase. "It's nearly time for dinner, and my daughter has not returned from the gardens yet." Lady Huntingdon drew near and Christian offered his arm. "Would you care to join my little search party?"

"I'm happy to help, my lady, but I have not freshened up after my journey." Christian let her take the lead as they strolled toward the back of the house.

"La, you can do that later. I've always loved the smell of leather and horses." She gave him a smile. "Did you have a pleasant ride?"

"I did." Christian stepped out onto the back terrace that boasted a wide path toward the estate gardens. "Does your daughter often lose track of time in the garden?"

"No. She's with Lord Pembroke at the moment," the duchess replied. "He arrived earlier this afternoon, and after some brief refreshment, he asked for a tour of the gardens." She looked up at Christian. "He must truly love flowers."

Christian's smile froze on his face. Flowers were probably the last thing Pembroke cared about. And Lady Alice had been giving him a tour. What if Pembroke was Thomas's murderer? He did have a long nose and light hair. His step lengthened slightly, wanting to find him and Alice as soon as possible. Thankfully, they weren't hard to spot, sitting on a bench with a maid nearby. They were obviously deep in conversation. What could they be talking about? Was Pembroke giving her the answers she'd tried to get at the ball?

The duchess seemed to sense his urgency and picked up her pace. They reached Alice's side quickly. "Alice, darling, it's nearly dinner, and you need time to get properly prepared." The duchess let go of Christian's arm. "You mustn't make her late, Lord Pembroke," she chided, then softened her words with a laugh.

Lord Pembroke gave Alice a warm look. "I wouldn't dream of making Lady Alice late. Shall we?" He winged out his elbow for her, but her mother stepped in and took his arm instead.

"I must know what you two have found so diverting," she said, looking back at her daughter. "Your faces were quite animated."

"I'd like to know as well," Christian said. Alice cast her eyes heavenward, but when she started after them, Christian held out his arm. "Allow me to escort you, my lady."

Her upbringing wouldn't allow her to reject his offer, but he did hear a soft sigh pass her lips before she took his arm. "Did you just arrive, my lord?" she asked, wrinkling her nose.

Christian leaned closer. "Is that your subtle way of telling me I should have refreshed myself before escorting your mother to the garden?"

"Perhaps." She looked away from him, toward the lake. "If you require some water right away, the lake is quite bracing this time of year."

"Do you know that from personal experience?" The top of her head was so close to his nose that the subtle scent of roses clinging to her hair wafted up to him.

"A lady would never divulge such information." She brought her eyes back to his, her heart-shaped face lit with warmth from the last rays of the sun dipping below the horizon. "I'm sure we'll be boating and picnicking on the lake during the house party. Do you swim, my lord?"

"Every nobleman is taught to swim." He slowed his step as they approached the house, not yet wanting to relinquish her.

"The Earl of Moreland's son wasn't. Isn't that curious?" She said it as if she were discussing the weather.

The words were like a bucket of cold water sluicing over him. She *had* been questioning Pembroke about Thomas's death. Christian schooled his face not to react. "Did Pembroke tell you that?" Christian looked at the man in question, who was impatiently waiting for them on the terrace. "How would he know such a detail? They weren't school chums, merely members of the same club."

"Lord Pembroke seems to be full of information." She kept her voice low, obviously not wanting their conversation to carry as they approached him.

"He's full of something," Christian muttered.

"He's quite distraught over Thomas's death." She glanced at the house. "There is room for doubt of his guilt."

"Is there? After what happened at the ball, you must take care, Alice. I don't like people shooting at you."

The duchess was waving them on, and Alice let go of his arm. "Who's to say they were shooting at *me*?" Her lips curved upward for a moment before it disappeared. "Don't worry about me, Lord Wolverton. I can take care of myself." Then the smile was back, as if the sun had broken through the clouds. "I'll see you at dinner," she said sweetly, gliding away and catching up to Lord Pembroke and her mother.

Christian watched her go, admiration mixed with frustration running through him. She was unlike any woman he'd ever met. Under better circumstances, he would be tempted to further their acquaintance for personal reasons. But for now, she needed him to stay close and offer his protection.

Whether she knew it or not.

CHAPTER 5

*A*lice was seated between Lord Pembroke and Lord Wolverton at dinner. It would have been the perfect opportunity to subtly question Pembroke, but the tension emanating from the two men was nearly palpable. She calmly took a bite of her poached salmon and smiled at the vicar, who sat across from her. There wasn't a polite way for Pembroke to confide his distress over Thomas and confess what their last conversation had been. If there had been, she might have had a more positive case for his innocence, especially if Wolverton was a witness to such a discussion. There was nothing for it, but to keep their conversation on approved topics while in company.

"Tell me, Lord Pembroke, will you be joining us for our picnic by the lake tomorrow?" Raising her fork, she took another small bite of fish. Her mother had carefully invited an even number of ladies and gentlemen for each day's planned diversion, so it would be a shame if anyone declined.

"Yes. Your mother has asked me to take charge of a boat. Dare I hope you will allow me the privilege of rowing you across the lake?" He smiled lazily at her, knowing she wouldn't refuse.

Clearly, Lord Pembroke had rarely been refused anything as had many of their class among the *ton*.

"I'd be delighted." Alice glanced toward the head of the table at her mother, who was watching her carefully, tilting her head toward the marquess. Alice couldn't be sure exactly what that meant. She looked to her right and was surprised when she met Christian's gaze.

"I hope the weather will hold for the picnic." Christian put his napkin on the table. "The days have been so mild lately, it makes me think that our fine weather will turn soon."

"Do you always anticipate negative events if there have been too many happy ones?" Alice's brows drew down, but her mouth lifted in a smile.

"Just planning for all contingencies, my lady." Christian leaned in. "In this instance, I think the odds may be in your favor. There's hardly a cloud in the sky."

"How fortunate," she murmured. He was so close, their shoulders touched, and his breath fanned across her cheek. His scent of bergamot and mint washed over her, the heat of his body magnifying it. Suddenly Lord Pembroke and the rest of the dinner guests seemed far away, and her vision tunneled down to just Christian. "Who would you like to partner with for the boat excursion?" she managed to get out. Had someone caught his eye? Would it bother her if they had?

"I believe my lady of choice is spoken for," he said quietly, shifting slightly closer to her. Alice's heart flipped at his words. Did he mean them?

"Perhaps I could ride along with you and Lord Pembroke?" Christian raised one eyebrow in question.

"The boats are made for only two," Pembroke answered, affecting a sad expression before giving Alice a smile. "I'm very much looking forward to spending time with you, Lady Alice."

She dipped her head, a small part of her disappointed that

Christian wouldn't be with her. But they were here to prove Pembroke's guilt or innocence as a murderer and possible traitor. She needed to focus on that and sharing a boat with him could yield the answers she was looking for.

"Have you ever been at sea?" Alice asked Pembroke. Maybe she could turn the conversation to details about him that might be useful later.

"Unfortunately, with the war, I wasn't able to travel or go on a Grand Tour. Now that it's over, however, I'd love to spend some time abroad," Pembroke said. He leaned his head forward in order to see Christian better. "What about you, Lord Wolverton? Do you like to travel for leisure?"

"Not particularly. I had my fill of living abroad during the war. Now that it's over, I find I appreciate British soil even more than before." He went back to eating his fish course, the subject obviously closed.

Alice wanted to know more about Christian. She knew very few details of his war service beyond the reports of valor in several battles. He'd commanded a battalion of men and seemed to be well-loved by them. But how had he received the small scars near his ear and eyebrow? She had so many questions that she couldn't politely ask.

The conversation lulled as the next course was brought out. Pembroke shifted in his seat, as if uncomfortable with the silence. "So, Wolverton, did you ever go to Tattersall's?" he asked while waiting for the servants to set the roast lamb and vegetables before him.

Christian picked up his glass of wine, holding it loosely in his hand. "No, I didn't have the time. I'd like to buy a new carriage to match the horses I'm considering buying, though. Tell me, when was the last time you purchased a new carriage? Do you have any advice on what to look for?"

The air around them was suddenly charged making Alice sit up straighter. What was Christian's purpose in asking after carriages? She looked at Pembroke who visibly swallowed.

"It's been some time since I purchased a carriage. I usually leave that up to one of the servants. Now, horseflesh I can advise you on. Next time we're both in Town, we can go together and look at what's available. Perhaps a nice set of matched grays would do." Pembroke cut into his meat and took a bite, chewing his food slowly.

"Do all of your carriages have the Pembroke crest on them? I wonder if I should take the time to have the Colborne crest applied to a new carriage or have one without." Christian speared a bite of lamb from his plate, but kept his eyes on Pembroke.

"My father proudly displayed our family crest on all our carriages." Pembroke turned to Alice and took a breath, obviously releasing some of the tension he'd held since Christian brought up the subject. "All this talk of horses and carriages must be so tedious for you. Let's change the subject to something more pleasing to a lady. Will you be favoring us with a musical selection this evening?"

"No, I think my mother has planned to have the performances tomorrow evening." She touched her napkin to her lips. "I believe Lady Beatrice and Miss Beasley will be performing as well, and I'm quite looking forward to it."

She looked down the table at the ladies in question. Lady Beatrice was just out of the schoolroom and still giggled a tad too loudly in company. She was speaking to the vicar's father on her right, who looked like he was fighting sleep. Miss Penelope Beasley was more forward and anxious to make a good match with a peer. Their eyes met across the table and Penelope gave her a weary smile. She was seated next to an older baron who had spoken of little besides his beloved hound dogs. Alice didn't know her well, but was looking forward to furthering their acquaintance during the house party. The person Alice was most looking forward to spending time with, however, was her best friend Elizabeth. She couldn't wait for her to arrive tomorrow. Elizabeth was like a sister to her and had a steadying hand Alice might need to get through the next few days.

As they were waiting for the dessert to be brought out, Christian put down his drink and turned toward Alice and Pembroke. "So, have either of you heard any more news about the inquiry into Thomas Norwich's death?"

Christian asked the question so bluntly, and yet casually, that it caught Alice off-guard. She glanced at Pembroke whose face had shuttered.

"No," he said flatly.

"I heard some new evidence has been found," Christian continued. "It sounded like they're closing in on a suspect."

Alice narrowed her eyes. If that was true, she would have been informed. Was he trying to scare Pembroke into revealing himself? "What new evidence would that be, my lord?"

"I'm not at liberty to say." Christian moved his knife and fork to the side of his now-empty plate so the servants could clear it away. "But I hope there will be an arrest soon. Thomas should get the justice he deserves."

Pembroke took a sip of his drink before he turned to Christian. "I agree. Justice should be served and the culprit punished. I was quite sad to hear of his passing. He was so young."

To Alice's ear, Pembroke sounded as sincere as he had in the garden, but Christian looked skeptical. In all of her conversations with Pembroke, he hadn't seemed secretive or upset, but perhaps Christian knew something she didn't. Hopefully she would get a chance to ask him later.

All too soon, it was time for the ladies to retire to the drawing room so the men could enjoy their port. The moment the door to the parlor closed, Lady Penelope came to Alice's side and sat down, clasping her hands in her lap.

"How lucky you are to have been seated next to a marquess *and* an earl," Penelope gushed. "Whatever did you talk about?"

Alice raised a hand as if waving away the question. "You know how gentlemen are. They talked of horses and carriages."

"My mother would love to see me further my acquaintance with both gentlemen," she said, lowering her voice. She twisted her hands and lifted her eyes to Alice's face. "I wonder if you would introduce me to Lord Wolverton first. He's so handsome."

A tiny stab of jealousy pricked Alice's heart, but she ignored it. "Of course," she replied. "I want all of our house guests to get acquainted. And there will be plenty of time throughout the next few days to converse and be partners with everyone at the party." They chatted about some of the fun activities the duchess had planned.

"I'm so glad the evening entertainments will include charades," Penelope said, biting her lip. "I'm especially good at it."

Alice smiled at her, glad that there was something for Penelope to look forward to. At that moment, the door opened, and the men joined them. Christian's eyes met hers, and an awareness arced between them as he started toward her. He looked so determined and handsome that her heart skipped a beat, and butterflies took flight in her middle. When had she allowed herself to indulge in an attraction to Christian Wolverton?

Her father stopped Christian before he could reach her, and soon they were in deep conversation. She should have been curious about what they were discussing, but instead she felt overheated. Deciding she needed a moment to collect herself, she stood and opened the balcony door so she could slip out. Gulping air as if she'd been swimming underwater, she leaned against the wall, enjoying the coolness of the stone against her back.

She wasn't alone for long. The door clicked open, and two sets of footsteps sounded on the stone, with the unmistakable scent of bergamot and mint wafting to her. Her father and Christian.

Straightening, she waited for them to turn toward her. "What's going on?" she asked. "Has something happened?"

"I had three peers in mind that had the means and access to that list, but two have alibis. That narrows the field considerably—to Lord Pembroke." Her father clasped his hands behind his back and gave Alice a pointed look. "Our agents are in place, watching for any other noblemen in Kent, as well as keeping our family and guests safe. I would still prefer that you and your mother not go anywhere unescorted, even on the grounds. We'll hold the masquerade ball as planned to lull him into false security that he could pass the list to his buyer anonymously there. If Pembroke is the traitor, we'll be ready for him. And hopefully catch the French buyer, as well." Her father turned to Christian. "I'd like to see you in my study after breakfast tomorrow."

"Of course, Your Grace." Christian looked between them. "Do you plan to go on with the house party as if there were nothing amiss?"

"Yes. I don't want to spook Pembroke. The buy must go on as planned." The duke touched Alice's shoulder. "It's risky, I know."

She gave him a reassuring smile. "With so many lives at stake, it can't be helped. Are there *any* other suspects to be considered?"

"Not right now, but if you have evidence of Pembroke's innocence, I'm eager to hear it."

She shook her head. There wasn't anything concrete yet.

Her father gave her a nod. "I'm going to join your mother. Don't be long." Her father kissed her forehead and went back inside.

Alice watched Christian go to the railing and look out over the gardens. What was he thinking? As if he could hear her thoughts, he turned to face her. His gaze lingered on her face. "Are you well?"

"I'm fine, my lord. I just needed a bit of air." She moved toward him, feeling a strange pull to be closer. He was quiet and contemplative this evening. She stood next to him, her skirt brushing his ankle. They both seemed to be looking at her favorite bench near the entryway of the maze garden. Had it only been a few hours ago that Christian had found her there with Pembroke?

The silence was comfortable, and the breeze was teasing her senses with the last scents of summer—scythed grass mixed with the fragrances of the garden. Alice closed her eyes, the familiar smells made new by the unfamiliar man standing beside her.

His voice broke through her thoughts. "Please, call me Christian."

She didn't turn. The thought of calling him by his given name was tantalizing. It would be highly improper, but she wanted to. Did she dare?

"Alice." His voice was gravelly. Compelling. It was easy to imagine him as a commander of an army, used to being obeyed.

"Yes?" She turned toward him, unable to resist admiring his evening attire. The blue waistcoat accented his eyes, making them appear to be the deep-blue of the sky right before it submits to the darkness of night.

His hand hovered over her upper arm, but didn't make contact. "I want you to know you can trust me."

His voice, deep and mesmerizing, made her think he was talking about something more than the business with Pembroke. Could he feel a connection to her like she did to him? "What do you mean?" She looked up into his face, and her eyes fell on those scars. Her hand lifted to touch one.

"Tell me what Pembroke has confided in you." His voice was still low, but he might as well have shouted, as his words jarred her senses.

The pull she'd felt toward him earlier snapped. That's what this was about, charming her so she would give him information. Oh, she'd heard the stories of him and his reputation for getting information. Now she'd experienced his power of influence for herself.

She stepped back. What was she thinking, letting his appeal cloud her judgment?

"Despite what you and my father say, I spoke to David in the garden, and I don't think he's Thomas's killer or our traitor." Putting her hands around her middle, she turned toward the railing, breaking the spell of his gaze.

"You call Pembroke by his given name now? Were you swayed by his handsome face?" He was at her back now, his mouth near her ear. Oh, how close he was to the truth. But it wasn't David Pembroke's handsome face she'd been swayed by.

"I am quite skilled at spotting a liar," she told him. "I believe he is telling the truth."

"Did he tell you that he wasn't allowed to serve in the war because he was the sole heir to the earldom? And that he was turned down for intelligence work? There's a good chance he's lashing out at those who were accepted into both the military and intelligence." He touched her shoulder and gently pressed her to face him. "The other two men your father suspected have alibis. We're almost sure it's Pembroke. Who else could it be?"

She looked up into his face, his blue eyes unfathomable, filled with so many secrets he'd known and kept. "The exchange is in two days. Our only recourse is to stick close to him and prove his guilt or innocence, as well as look for any other possible suspects."

"Then the masquerade will be a day of reckoning for all of us." He leaned away from her, and she heard him sniff. "Do you smell that?'

Alice sniffed as well. She pushed past him and leaned over the railing. Smoke curled into the sky, and men were beginning to shout.

"The stables are on fire. We've got to get the horses out. Now."

CHAPTER 6

*C*hristian wiped the soot out of his eyes, his once-white lawn shirt now blackened and gray. Luckily, the stable hands and groomsmen had leapt into action, and most of the stable fire had been contained to the tack room—a near miracle. It would be much easier for the duke to replace equipment than a valuable animal.

Walking back toward the drive, Christian looked around the lawn at the servants, family members, and guests who had gathered to watch. He found a cluster of maids surrounding the duchess and several houseguests, but when Christian's gaze searched the faces, Alice's wasn't among them. His stomach dropped. She hadn't gone near the stables, had she?

Turning on his heel, he strode back toward the smoldering side of the stables. Groomsmen still poured buckets of water on the structure. Alice wasn't there. Could the fire have been a distraction to spirit her away? Or worse?

Turning in frustration and worry, he finally saw a lone woman a short distance away, her figure familiar. Her arms were folded as she stared at the burned section of the stables. He started toward her, relieved she was safe.

When he reached her side, she looked up at him, not with sadness, as he'd expected, but calm determination. "This isn't a coincidence."

"No, it isn't." He stood next to her and they watched the last embers sizzling as the servants poured water over the wood.

"We're lucky we didn't lose any servants or horses. We very nearly did." She dropped her arms to her side and started walking back toward the house. "I need to find my father."

"He was directing the water brigade on the south side of the stables so no embers will burst into flame there." He easily kept pace with her. "Do you have a theory as to who might be behind this?"

"Possibly." She glanced over at him and briefly pursed her lips. "But I need more facts."

They reached the graveled drive that led to the house when the Duke of Huntingdon approached them. His own coat was smudged with soot and his brow was drawn down in concern. "Pearce saw a man running away from the stables just before the fire broke out. He ran him down, and there was a scuffle. Pearce was stabbed, and the suspected arsonist ran in the direction of the village."

Christian's pulse picked up at the mention of Pearce. "How bad is Pearce's injury? Will he recover?"

"I'm not sure. My personal physician has been called." The duke's face was grim. "We're going after the man responsible. Would you care to find a mount and join us?"

"Yes," both Christian and Alice replied simultaneously. Christian was surprised by her answer. Surely the duke wouldn't let her accompany them. Yet when he turned toward the paddock where the horses had been moved, she did as well. He put his hand on her arm. "Perhaps you should stay here and oversee Pearce's care. It's nearing dark, my lady."

Her eyes narrowed and she frowned. "And darkness or daylight, I know this land far better than you, *my lord*." She faced him with a stubborn set to her jaw.

"Enough!" the duke said from their right, his voice like a crack of gunfire. His hand sliced through the air. "We'll need Alice's ability as a guide and Wolverton's as a tracker. Both of you get a horse saddled. We'll leave immediately."

Christian shook his head, but didn't say more. He offered an arm to escort her to the paddock, but she brushed by without a second glance. Wryly, he followed.

Several grooms had their hands full trying to calm the horses, who were stamping and nervous, though the groomsmen were able to get two horses saddled with tack that had been saved from the fire. Alice kept her arms folded, staring past the stables toward the edges of her family's property. Her evening dress was still mostly presentable, though she wasn't wearing her gloves. She looked ready to sit down to dinner. Instead, she was getting ready to ride out after the man who had stabbed Pearce.

Christian didn't mind the lack of conversation. He still wasn't sure how he felt about Alice's status with the Falcon Group, and he was organizing his own thoughts about what the arson meant. In the last seventy-two hours, an agent had been killed, an attempt made on his or Alice's life, arson, and now an agent had been stabbed. Was the traitor trying to kill agents on the list before he sold their names to the French? Or distract them from the exchange? And it hadn't escaped his attention that Pembroke had been present at every incident. Though Christian could only assume he was still at the house, since he hadn't seen Pembroke on the grounds or near those putting out the fire. Where was he really? Was he the suspected arsonist running toward the village?

When Christian and Alice were both mounted and ready, the

duke and several grooms on horseback motioned for them to turn toward the east side of the estate. "We'll search in pairs," the duke announced. "Fire one shot into the air if you find the blackguard."

Christian instinctively maneuvered his horse close to Alice's, and she didn't seem to mind. They broke off from the group, which was fanning out on the edges of the property that led to the village and headed toward the center of a wooded area. The last vestiges of light were quickly fading, and they didn't have much time before blackness would envelop them.

Christian followed Alice's horse as they galloped to the wood. Slowing, they picked their way over fallen logs and around tree limbs, cautiously moving forward until they came to a small clearing. Alice slid off her horse, and Christian did the same. He immediately saw several low-hanging branches that had been bent. A tell-tale sign showing someone had been through here. He leaned over to look at them.

"What do you see?" she asked, her voice low.

He pulled a branch forward to show her. "It's freshly broken. Someone has passed this way recently." He tied his horse's reins to the more sturdy branches on the other side and reached for Alice's horse to tie hers as well.

Christian peered around the clearing. The man could be hiding anywhere in this wood or gone on his way to the village. "Let's see if we can pick up his trail."

He walked forward, looking for any tracks or signs that someone had run by. Nothing. Alice had moved a dozen steps to his right, both of them on alert for any hint of the intruder. The deeper they went into the trees, the darker it became.

He turned to suggest that they go back to the horses, when he saw a man dressed in dark clothing appear out of the trees, running straight toward Alice. He was hardly more than a shadowy blur. Christian bolted toward them, but he was too late. The assailant tackled her, rolling with her to the ground. The darkness of the foliage and shrubbery seemed to swallow them up, and Christian felt like a blind man stumbling about as he tried to find them.

"Alice!" he shouted.

He heard her cry out and then a man's choking roar. Heading toward the sounds, he saw a shadow crashing through the forest in front of him. The man was getting away, but all Christian could think of was Alice. He rushed to her side, where she was crouched near a tree stump, holding her stomach.

"Are you hurt?" He pulled her to him, pushing her hair away from her face. "Alice?"

"I'm well," she said automatically, but her voice was shaky. He gently took her by the shoulders to look over her person and felt stickiness on his hands. Blood. As his eyes adjusted, he could see dark stains all over the front of her dress.

"You're bleeding," he said, his heart hammering in his chest. He needed to get her to a doctor immediately. He froze, wanting to sweep her onto his horse and ride hard back to the house, but his innate sense of direction had disappeared. He wasn't sure where to find his horse.

"No, the blood isn't mine," she said, looking down at her clothing. "He had a knife, but when he raised it, I was able to twist around and then . . . " She took a deep breath. "I stabbed him. It's his blood," she finally said.

Relief flooded Christian. He stopped resisting his instincts and bent to pick her up, needing to hold her for a moment and reassure himself that she was well. "We'll talk more when we get back to the estate."

She put her hand up to stop him. "I'm perfectly capable of walking," she protested. He set her down as requested, but when her foot touched the ground, she cried out.

Christian lifted her once again and held her to his chest. "Allow me."

She was as still as a granite statue in his arms as he carried her back to the horses. "I stabbed him," she said softly.

He could hear the shock in her voice. "You did what you had to do. Could you see his face?" He adjusted her weight, pulling her a little closer and letting her soft curls rest on his cheek. She seemed fragile all of a sudden, and he didn't like that feeling. Since he'd met her, she'd been strong and challenging. He liked thinking of her that way. *Needed* her to stay that way.

"Not really." She finally laid her head on his shoulder as if the weight she was carrying was too much to bear at the moment. All too soon they reached the horses and it was time to let her go. He lifted her onto the saddle and waited until she was settled. "We'll find him."

She stared down at him from atop the horse, determination in her gaze. "Next time we'll be ready."

He liked that she used "*we*," but it twisted the guilt flowing through him at the same time. He nodded and reluctantly left her side to mount his own horse. Once he was in the saddle, he stayed within arm's reach of Alice the entire ride back to Langdon Park, making sure she didn't jostle her injured foot.

Even though it was near dark, he couldn't wait for her to change out of that torn and bloody dress. It only reminded him of how close she'd come to losing her life. Again. At the ball, she'd run toward danger, and this time, danger had run toward her. He'd been mere feet away both times, and both times he'd been unable to stop it. Whoever this was had caught Christian off-guard twice, and Alice had nearly paid with her life. That wouldn't happen again.

He looked over at her, with her back straight and hair falling around her waist. Her chin was raised, and she appeared as a warrior approaching the castle with her battle wounds. Yes, Alice Huntingdon was a fighter, and she was someone he'd fight beside.

Because together, he knew they could win.

CHAPTER 7

*A*lice breathed in the early morning air as the sun began its work of melting away the mist from the ground. The birds were singing in the trees, and the beauty of it all soothed her soul. The only thing to mar her view had been the gaping black hole where the tack room had once stood. At least the horses were safe and the grooms were able to keep the animals calm.

She'd tried to look in on the stable hand that had been stabbed last night, but the doctor had given him an extra dose of laudanum, so he was expected to sleep until later this afternoon. She'd hoped to be able to question him, but she had other areas to investigate while she waited. After finding her favorite horse, Dolly, and feeding her the apple she'd brought, Alice took the time to brush her down before their ride. It was time well spent that was therapeutic for both of them, and something Alice desperately needed.

In addition to the events of last night, Alice had received news this morning that her best friend Elizabeth would be unable to attend the house party. Her father had chosen a man for her to marry and was requiring her to stay in London for the entire courtship. Worry for Elizabeth had immediately washed over Alice. Elizabeth's father wasn't kind and the chance was high that he'd chosen a man who wouldn't ever hold his daughter's heart. Alice wanted to hurry back to London and support her friend, but finding that list of agent names before it was sold was her first priority. With a deep sigh, Alice stepped on the mounting block and settled herself in the saddle. The moment she could go to Elizabeth, she would.

She rolled her neck as Dolly walked down the path that led to the wood. She was still sore from being attacked last night. Even after a long, hot bath before bed, her muscles had protested when she'd gotten up this morning. Her ankle still pained her, but not as badly as last night. At least she could put some weight on it today. Lacing her half boot up tighter than normal seemed to help. Now she wanted to go back to the wood and see if the man had left behind a clue to his identity.

Spurring Dolly into a gallop across the slope of the park, she only slowed when they reached the edge. When the thunder of hoofbeats sounded behind her, she turned, unsurprised to see Christian. He quickly caught up, his hair windblown and a grin on his face. "I didn't think to see you up and about so early, my lady."

"You think me a slug-a-bed?" She tilted her head in her horse's direction. "I don't think Dolly would forgive me if I missed our morning ride."

"She is a beautiful horse." He leaned forward in the saddle. "Though I was thoroughly impressed by the mount your stable master chose for me today. Did your father name him?"

"No, but the duke finds it comical to be outranked by a horse." Alice smiled. "He usually rides Prince himself."

"I hope he won't mind that I borrowed him." Christian patted the horse's neck and Prince snorted as if giving his consent.

"I'm sure he won't." Alice took a moment to admire how Christian sat a horse, strong and confident, his broad shoulders as powerful as the horse's beneath him— as if he was born to ride.

He looked over at her and she felt a flush creeping up her cheeks. His lips curved, and Alice was grateful he was not a mind reader.

"Might I inquire as to where your groom is, my lady? I'm sure your father doesn't allow you to ride without an escort." Christian turned as if a chaperone would appear like a wraith in the mist.

Alice looked over at him, amused at his antics. "Don't worry, my lord, I am safe from anyone who has designs on my person. Henry, my groom, is never far behind, and he generally keeps me in view. He doesn't like to intrude, so he stays a respectable distance behind."

Christian frowned and his brows drew together, all merriment fleeing at her words. "Is that safe? Especially now with the case we're working on directly targeting agents. If something happened, he might not be close enough to help you."

Alice tightened her grip on the reins. "I'm not going far, and I'm armed."

He cocked his head and slowly looked over her person. Alice fought the urge to squirm under his gaze and raised her chin at his perusal.

"Would it be improper to ask where you are hiding the weapon?" he finally said with a broad grin.

"Yes, it would." The corners of her mouth lifted as he carefully looked over her riding habit one more time. She'd altered all her clothing to conceal a knife sheathed at her waist, but it was very hard to spot. Not that Christian wasn't trying. He could be quite incorrigible.

Her smile faded, though, when she looked ahead to the little wooded area in front of them. She took a breath to calm her heart. "If I were to guess, we are both out here for the same reason."

Christian followed her gaze. "I believe so." He dismounted and came to her side. "May I help you down, my lady?"

"If you would, please."

He reached up, settling his hands around her waist before he helped her to the ground. "You're hoping there's a clue to the man's identity that we couldn't see in the darkness of the trees last night."

"Yes." Her tongue seemed thick, and she shook out her skirts to cover how disconcerted she was by his closeness. His now-familiar scent of bergamot and mint filled her nostrils, and she could feel the warmth of his body through her riding habit. His nearness multiplied the few butterflies she'd already been dealing with into a rioting mob of them.

Quickly stepping away, she busied herself with tying Dolly's reins to a nearby tree. "Stay here, girl," she murmured as Dolly inspected the grass below her. "I won't be long."

Christian did the same for his horse and they walked into the woods together. The familiar trees looked different in the daylight, with sunshine filtering through the branches. She'd walked these woods as a girl, climbing the trees and finding all the best hiding places. But last night had changed things.

Her stomach tightened, remembering the attacker's hands reaching for her throat, the feel of the knife piercing his shoulder. The truth was, she'd hardly been able to sleep last night, going over the scene again and again in her mind. Yes, she'd been trained in how to use knives, daggers, and swords, but that was the first time she'd actually stabbed someone to save her own life. The experience had shaken her far more than she'd thought possible.

She could feel Christian's gaze on her. Wanting to appear unaffected so he wouldn't think her unequal to the task ahead, she took a deep breath and kept moving forward. The broken branches and flattened grasses clearly showed where she had been tackled. Pushing down the memory, she walked closer and bent down to see if anything had fallen out of the man's pockets or if any clues had been left behind. Christian crouched beside her.

"You hide your emotions well, but you don't need to when you're with me," he said softly. "I know that what happened last night was . . . difficult."

"I'm conducting an investigation." Despite the turmoil inside, Alice was able to keep her voice level. If she spoke of her innermost feelings, she might cry. That would lead to a discussion she'd heard often among male counterparts— that women belonged in the home and not in the field. She couldn't bear to hear Christian say she shouldn't do her job. She had to appear professional.

There was a streak of blood on the grass, but no obvious blood trail. Standing, she took a step toward the bushes straight ahead. The scratches on her arms attested to those brambles being the ones she'd gotten caught in. If only she'd had her gloves, her skin would have been better protected. But she hadn't put them back on before she'd joined the search party. Her hands instinctively rubbed her arms, as if she were cold.

Christian was right behind her, and she was aware of his every movement. He reached out and touched her shoulder. "Alice."

He said her given name so intimately, as if he had the right to use it. His voice wove a spell of security around her. His presence filled the spaces, the holes that fear had drilled into her heart. How did he know exactly what she needed? Maybe he was different. Maybe she really could trust him.

She turned to face him and took his hand in hers, drawing it down between them, intertwining their fingers. "I'm well."

He lifted her gloved hand to his lips and kissed the back of it, keeping his eyes on hers. "I believe you."

Just moments ago she'd wished to have her gloves on last night, but at the moment she wished her hands were gloveless. His kiss had sparked tingles all the way up her arm.

She stood speechless for another heartbeat, watching him,

hearing his words echo through her mind and heart. He believed her. Believed *in* her. "Thank you."

He let out a breath, seemingly as affected at the emotions swirling around them as she was. His voice was low and sure. "You know, if you'd been in the army, you would have had the commiseration of every officer around you to help you get through this. The bond between you would have become unbreakable when you shared what happened. Once you experience battle together, you become part of a unique circle of brotherhood that can be a shelter and protection."

He'd stepped closer, the buttons on his jacket nearly touching the front of her riding habit. Alice's heart sped up at the way he looked at her. "But I'm not a man, so I couldn't be part of a brotherhood, my lord," she said, a trifle breathless.

"At this moment, I'm grateful you're not a man." He lifted his hand and touched her cheek, letting it trail down her jaw. "I want you to be in *my* circle, Alice. Let me help shoulder your burden."

Their connection stretched and pulled between them, beckoning her to lean on his strength and coaxing her to share. "Have you ever . . . stabbed someone?" she asked softly, looking up at him.

"Yes." His face was solemn. Even the birds stopped singing, as if they were all holding their breath to hear his answer. "I'd been sent near the frontline for my first battle, and I saw the man's face in my dreams for a month. But I did what I had to do to survive, just as you did last night."

Tears pricked the back of her eyelids, but she pressed them closed. She would not cry. "I've practiced and trained, but I wasn't prepared to feel a knife puncture flesh at my own hand." She touched her throat, feeling her attacker's fingers there once more. "He had quite large hands."

Christian's jaw clenched before he reached out to capture her hand in his. "Your training was superb, Alice. Pearce was also a trained agent, one of the best. He was stabbed, but you weren't. That's something to be proud of, though not many people will ever be privileged to know of it."

"Yes, that isn't a topic I can broach at a morning call. Such a thing would definitely set tongues to wagging." She smiled at the very idea. It felt good to be with him and discuss things she'd only ever talked about with her father.

"I hope you know you can talk about it with me. Anytime." He set his hands on her shoulders. Though he was standing a little closer than propriety demanded, Alice didn't step away. She had to admit, the look in his eyes gave her an extra bit of confidence that she hadn't known she lacked.

Christian cleared his throat. "I was thinking last night that with all that you've been through recently, you must have a variety of colorful bruises on your person. You fell on the terrace at the ball, and then the fall last evening as well." He tilted his head and let his fingers lightly brush down her arms and back to her shoulders, and she shivered at his touch. "And yet here you are, out in the woods, investigating."

Alice was determined to keep her equilibrium while he was near, but she had to admit it was more difficult than she'd thought. Her hand went instinctively to her hip. "I do have some bruises, yes, but I believe it highly improper to speak of them. Luckily my maid has a poultice that draws out the pain." She smiled and motioned toward his temple. "And since we're asking improper questions about injuries, I've been wondering, did you receive your scars in a knife fight?"

He lifted a hand and touched the now-white scars near his ear. "Yes. A surprise attack. I moved just in time to avoid my throat being sliced and got these instead."

She winced. That had been awfully close then. "You were lucky not to have been killed."

"Very." He ran a hand over his jaw. "The scars are so faded now, I'm surprised you noticed them." He arched a brow. "And mentioned it out loud."

She pulled her shoulders to her ears and winced a little. "Yes, I know. My mother would give me an hour-long comportment lecture if she knew I mentioned a war hero's scar in conversation, but as we are throwing all polite conversation topics to the wind today, I had to satisfy my curiosity." She shouldn't be asking these questions, but she couldn't stop herself. And it had been a welcome distraction from remembering the details of the stabbing.

"I seem to recall warning you about how dangerous curiosity can be." He shook his head, a suitably mournful expression on his face. "I didn't think you heeded me then."

"You're right, I didn't." She laughed. "My governess encouraged curiosity. She said it was the foundation of learning. And I am always learning, therefore I am always curious. I couldn't stop it any more than I could reverse the direction of the Thames."

He groaned aloud, but she knew he wasn't serious. Facing the bramble, she felt lighter, the heavy emotions gone. She had Christian to thank for that.

When she pushed forward, she saw a small piece of black fabric on one of the branches and stepped closer. After she plucked it off, Alice turned to show it to Christian. Rubbing it between her fingers, she made an assessment. "The man last night was dressed in black, so this most likely belongs to him. It's not a coarse fabric. Possibly lawn or cambric."

"So he has fine clothing." Christian pushed the frontmost branch away to get to something a little farther in the bush. "And he has blonde hair." He held up some strands of hair to the sunlight.

Alice sighed inwardly. The clues were leading in one direction only.

"From the look on your face, I know you're thinking it, so I'll just say it. Pembroke has blonde hair and fine clothing. His claims of sleeping through the stable fire are ludicrous at best. He could have easily been the arsonist last night, or at least an accomplice."

He was right, but she couldn't believe it. Pembroke had been sincere when she'd questioned him about Thomas. "This is all very circumstantial. Half the men in England have blonde hair and fine clothing."

"But half of England aren't suspects in our case." He looked down at her, his eyes searching. "Why do you want him to be innocent?"

"Why do *you* want him to be guilty?" she countered. With a shake of her head, she fixed her gaze on the bush and sighed. "I haven't drawn any conclusions, not really. I just want to have more proof than a few hairs and a piece of black fabric."

"We've got more proof than that." He held up his fingers and started counting off. "He was at the ball when the gunman was in the garden. He was there when the stables were set on fire. And it's possible he attacked you last night. You didn't see his face, but did you recognize his build? Or his voice?" Christian bent his head to look at the bush with her again. There wasn't anything else. Alice turned away.

"It all happened so fast. He had me on the ground. I felt the tip of his knife on my neck and tried to twist it out of his hand. He was choking me. I stabbed him. Then you were there." She tried to remember any other details. "He was taller than I, but I can't say if he was Pembroke's size. And if it *was* him last night, he didn't receive any wound treatment from our servants or staff. We would have heard about it."

"He could have hidden that." Christian scanned the other trees nearby. "We'll get more information. We've still got a little time to prove it's him."

They walked back to the horses. Alice was glad to leave the

scene behind. "Are you looking forward to the picnic?" she asked, hoping to change the subject. "It should be diverting."

"I'm sure it will be," he said, swishing a stick through the overgrowth at their feet. "But the novelty of eating outside was ruined for me by the army."

She chuckled. "Yes, I suppose that would do it. Was the food very bad?"

"It was, but we made the best of it. Seeing the poverty of the people in Spain made me grateful for the little we did have. There was so much suffering."

His voice was far away, and Alice wanted to call him back. She touched his sleeve. "I'm sure you did the best you could under the circumstances."

He tipped his head, obviously deep in thought, but didn't say anything until they reached the horses. "I want to go back someday, and see how the people have rebuilt their country and their lives. The Spanish are some of the most resilient people I've ever known. If anyone could rebuild, they can."

In that moment, Alice saw a side of Christian Wolverton that she was sure he didn't show to the world. Yes, he was a strategist, a spy, and someone who had fought and killed during the war. But darkness hadn't truly touched his soul. He still looked for the light and goodness that could come out of such a horrific experience. That was a strength not many men had.

"I hope you get to see Spain again in happier times," she said, as she untied her horse's reins. She was looking forward to the ride back, happy to be able to sit for a short while. Her ankle was starting to throb. "But first, my lord, we have a traitor to catch and a picnic to attend."

"What a harsh taskmaster you are," he said as he helped her onto her horse. His hands lingered on her waist for a moment. "In the army, I might have chafed under such direct orders, but with you, I find I don't mind as much."

Her heart skipped a beat as she looked down into the depths of his dark-blue eyes. The curve of his lips indicated he was teasing her, but the intensity of his gaze said there was an element of truth to what he was saying. She wasn't sure what to make of that.

"Get used to it," she said with a smile of her own, before she urged her horse homeward.

CHAPTER 8

Christian strolled slowly to the lake, the happy conversation of the other guests floating through the air. He pulled at his collar, careful not to muss his cravat. Miss Penelope Beasley had been partnered with him for this outing, and she had kept up a steady commentary on the current fashions and the gowns she'd had made for the house party. All that was required of him was to nod at regular intervals, which left him free to focus on Alice. Something had changed between them in the wood that morning. Their thread of connection had become something much stronger, and the pull toward her was becoming hard to resist.

And he was finding that he didn't want to.

He watched Pembroke help her into the boat, intent on rowing her to the privacy of the small island that boasted a Roman folly. Alice glanced his way, and when their gazes locked, she smiled and tilted her head in acknowledgment. Their growing attachment seemed mutual and Christian was glad of it. He'd never met a woman who'd captivated him so thoroughly.

She sat down in the boat and turned her attention back to

Pembroke. He was nervous, wiping his hands on his breeches before taking out a handkerchief and mopping his brow. Something was definitely troubling the man, and Christian had no doubt Alice could ferret the cause out of him. Christian just wanted to stay close and offer any assistance she might need.

"Are you ready for our boat excursion?" he asked the woman at his side, lengthening his stride a bit to get to the edge of the lake and not be far behind Alice.

"Of course, my lord," she said, hurrying to keep pace with him.

He stepped to the next available boat and held out his hand to help Miss Beasley into it. She was quite unsteady and it took several moments before she was settled. The second she was, he climbed in as well, taking the oars in his hands, while a footman pushed them into the water.

He started off at a leisurely pace, keeping Alice and Pembroke in his view. She was wore a fetching blue walking dress with a matching bonnet that framed her face just enough to leave room for a few curls to escape. He remembered how soft those curls had been against his cheek as he'd carried her to the horses after the attack. He'd been quite tempted to remove his gloves this morning to touch them again and see if his memory did them justice, but had decided against it. Touching her hair might have led to wanting to kiss her, and that wouldn't do.

Pulling back on the oars, he concentrated on Alice's gestures and mannerisms to gauge how well her questioning was going. So far she looked quite relaxed and at ease with Pembroke's conversation. He wished he were closer so he could witness her questioning skills. She was quite genius to use her standing in society to gather intelligence. No one would suspect a duke's daughter of passing along details she gathered during *ton* events.

Miss Beasley watched him from beneath the brim of her bonnet. "I was so pleased to be partnered with you today, my lord.

The weather is exceedingly fine." She gave him a bright smile and twirled her parasol half a turn.

Christian smiled politely. There were few topics of conversation that were appropriate for society events, and evidently they'd exhausted the fashions of the day and were moving on to the weather. Society hadn't changed a bit since he'd left for war. "It is very fine weather we're having," he agreed.

"I'm glad there's no wind to rock the boat. As pretty as it looks, I'm ever so afraid of the water," she said, looking at the side of the boat. "I hope we shan't tip over."

Christian raised his eyebrows at the implication that he couldn't efficiently row a small boat, but she was staring at the water as if it might suddenly attack her. "I won't let anything happen to you, my lady," he assured her.

He glanced over at Pembroke and Alice. She was smiling, trailing her hand along in the water, and Pembroke was watching her closely. Did his shoulder pain him while rowing? Part of Christian wanted to confront the man and force him to prove whether he had indeed been the one Alice had wounded in the wood. But the duke wanted to draw out the French buyer along with the traitor, so, for now, he had to be satisfied with this cat-and-mouse game.

"Have you ever seen a more picturesque view?" Miss Beasley asked. "Langford Park is quite pleasing to the eye. And how wonderful that the duke added a Roman folly to the island for a bit of flair. Very stylish for his generation."

"Yes, quite." Christian kept up the steady rowing pace to the island, but glanced back at the Park. It really was quite beautiful. "I'm partial to Northfield Hall, my family's country seat, though we do not boast a folly."

Miss Beasley giggled and twirled her parasol again. "I'm sure you could add one if you wished, my lord."

"Yes, of course." He looked beyond Miss Beasley's shoulder and watched Pembroke help Alice out of the boat. She was still limping slightly, but Pembroke didn't seem to notice. How much pain was she truly trying to hide? Regardless, he had to admire her tenacity. She wasn't letting anything interfere with the investigation.

"The breeze from the water is heavenly, don't you agree?" Miss Beasley leaned forward to catch his eye.

He pulled his attention from Alice and focused on Miss Beasley. "It is quite nice."

"Perhaps you wouldn't mind another turn about the lake so we can enjoy it." She was clutching the edge of her seat with one hand as if she couldn't wait to get to land, but looked at him in expectation of staying on the water.

Christian couldn't contradict a lady, so he smiled politely and bent to the task of angling the boat away from the island. This was going to be the fastest turn about the lake ever seen at Langford Park. Not only for Miss Beasley's peace of mind, but because Pembroke had offered Alice his arm, and they would soon disappear around the bend that led to the folly. He would lose sight of them. Though Alice could take care of herself, he didn't want her to be alone with the man who may have attacked her the evening before and had caused Alice such distress this morning.

As if Lord Pembroke could read his thoughts, his gaze left Alice's face for a moment and searched the guests who were close to the island. When his eyes met Christian's, Pembroke gave him a curt nod and then smiled down at Alice, pulling her closer to his side as they moved out of sight.

Christian barely contained a growl. What message was Pembroke trying to send? Was he courting Alice, or planning her demise as an agent to the Crown? Either option was unacceptable.

Stretching his arms, he rowed in a large half-turn before returning to the landing that would lead them to Pembroke and Alice. Once they had reached dry ground, he got out and pulled the boat more securely ashore. Miss Beasley released a small sigh, obviously relieved.

Christian held out his arm. "May I escort you to the folly?" he asked.

Miss Beasley reached for him, but stumbled as she was disembarking, and Christian barely managed to catch her before she ended up in the mud.

"Oh!" she cried out, looking up at him with wide, blue eyes. "You've saved me from a terrible fall, my lord." Her lower lip started to tremble. "I was so afraid of ruining my new gown, but you were my hero."

"I often vanquish any mud that tries to splatter on a lady." He gently helped her to an upright position until she was standing on her own two feet.

She giggled again. "A noble knight coming to my rescue."

"As any gentleman would." He gave her an exaggerated bow, and she laughed.

She took his arm once again, and they started up the path. "You are very different from what I imagined, my lord."

"Oh?" He gave her a sidelong glance. "How so?"

"I expected someone with your rank to be more reserved and unapproachable, but you are quite amiable," she admitted. A shade of pink touched her cheeks. "I hope it's not improper to say so."

Christian drew his brows down and shook his finger. "Miss Beasley, you must go on thinking me reserved and unapproachable. I have a reputation to protect." His lips curved in a half-smile. "Anything to the contrary shall be our secret."

She giggled again and leaned closer. "Of course, my lord. Your secret is safe with me."

They were approaching a bend in the only path that led down to the folly and Christian felt his neck prickle. That could only mean one thing. They were being watched. He could feel it. But by whom?

Scanning the crowds, he didn't see anyone out of place. A gaggle of servants stood on the shore near the older guests who hadn't come on the boat excursion. But no one seemed to be paying particular attention to them. Yet, Christian had learned long ago to trust his instincts. Someone was watching them. Closely.

Quickening their pace, he steered Miss Beasley down the path. He wanted Alice in his sight. Now.

CHAPTER 9

$\mathcal{A}$lice could sense the change in Pembroke from the moment she'd taken his arm to go down to the boat. He'd seemed nervous, though he was trying valiantly to hide it. She'd done her best to keep up the appearance of ease in conversation until they crested the hill that led down to the folly on the island and had a moment of privacy.

When they were alone, she squeezed his arm, keeping her steps slow and steady. "Is everything all right, my lord? You don't seem yourself today."

He let out a great sigh. "I'm not surprised you noticed that I'm a bit out of sorts. I didn't sleep well last night after my valet informed me of the stable fire. I rose when it was yet dark and stumbled over a chair and fell." He grimaced and rubbed his right elbow. "I think rowing might have injured it further."

"Perhaps we should call my father's physician." She stared at his elbow. Last night she'd wounded her attacker on his right shoulder. Could Pembroke be hiding that injury with a story about his elbow? "Dr. Stenbridge is quite talented in healing." And he could check Pembroke's shoulder during his examination if her father asked.

"I wouldn't want to trouble a physician. It's just an ache that is already improving." He held out his other elbow to help her up the small step inside the folly. The raised gazebo-like structure boasted several marble columns. "Though there is something I'd like to talk to you about, my lady."

Alice could hear laughter echoing from the guests still on the lake. Christian couldn't be far behind them. She'd felt his gaze on her several times this afternoon, and she'd had a hard time not looking his way. Pembroke led her to a bench on the left, which offered a bit of shade.

"What is it?" she asked, smoothing her skirts.

"It's a topic somewhat difficult to talk about, but I feel I must." Pembroke took out his handkerchief again to wipe the drops of sweat gathering on his forehead. He couldn't meet her gaze.

Alice's throat tightened. From his demeanor, whatever he was about to confess wasn't going to be pleasant. Could he be the traitor, as Christian thought and would he confess as much to her? "Whatever it is, you can tell me."

Her thoughts raced. The masquerade was tomorrow, but if he confessed today, the intrigue would be over, and the Falcon Group safe— but Pembroke would be tried as a traitor. Could she have been so wrong about his innocence? It was hard to imagine, though she was acutely aware she wasn't infallible.

Pembroke was looking toward the wood, his brow furrowed. "It's such a beautiful day; it doesn't seem proper to spoil it with something difficult."

Alice touched his hand. "What's wrong?"

"I know you've heard whispers about me. I was the last to see Thomas Norwich alive." He stopped and ran a hand through his hair. "We had words that night, but it wasn't what the gossipmongers are saying. You see, Thomas had come across an investment with a spice ship. A high return was almost guaranteed, and the captain had a sound record of delivering the promised goods. Thomas had made a tidy sum from the last shipment and thought to offer me the same opportunity."

"But I heard that the conversation between you was most heated. A good investment would be cause for celebration. Did you speak of anything else?" So far, nothing untoward had been confessed, but he obviously had more to tell.

Pembroke closed his eyes briefly before looking at her. "The ship sank, and we lost everything. Thomas had come to tell me the news. I was devastated." He ducked his head, as if he didn't want to tell her any more, but was determined to go on. "My estate is in need of funds, and I was counting on that shipment to provide it. When I realized all the money I'd invested was gone, with no hope of a return . . . I was angry."

"So, what happened then?" Alice gently prodded. People would be coming down the path any moment and their moment of privacy would end. She had to know.

"I'd just come from the club, mind you, and was a bit foxed. I grabbed his shoulders and shouted that I would lose everything. He backed up and made his apologies, said he wished there were something he could do. He'd lost a lot of money in the venture as well. He said he had a way to find out about more investments and that he'd get us another. I shook him, hard, and said I had nothing left. Nothing. And I took my leave." His eyes raised to hers. "He was alive and hailing a hackney when I last saw him. I didn't kill him. I need you to know that."

Alice watched him closely. He seemed so sincere. His breathing was steady, his voice was, as well, and he held just the right amount of eye contact. Every instinct she had told her he was being truthful. "I believe you." Despite the evidence piling up against him, Pembroke could very well be innocent.

He let out a long breath as if a large weight had been lifted from his shoulders. "Everyone looks at me differently now. Ladies whisper behind their fans when I enter a ballroom. I know there are some who go so far as to accuse me of murder. To hear you say that you believe me . . . I cannot tell you how much that means to me." He took her hand and drew it to his lips. "Though I do not deserve the company of a lady such as yourself, I'm grateful that you are here with me now." He kissed her knuckles and then clutched her hand to his heart. "And I hope we have many more moments like these."

Alice was deciding how best to respond when she felt a stir of energy surround her. Christian was near.

"There you are, Lady Alice. We've found you at last." Christian's voice was all that was polite, but she knew him well enough to hear the thread of tension underneath his words. She squeezed Pembroke's hand before she turned to greet Christian.

"How wonderfully clever of you to have found us. The shade of the trees on this side of the folly is such a relief from the heat." Alice tried to pull her hand away from Pembroke, but he gripped her tightly. She gave him a reassuring smile before wiggling her fingers. He released her, but his gaze lingered as she turned away. "And how are you enjoying the day, Miss Beasley?"

"It's been magnificent. Lord Wolverton took me on an extra turn about the lake so we could feel the breeze awhile longer." Miss Beasley looking into Christian's eyes, her adoration evident. "He also saved me from a terrible fall."

Alice raised a brow. "Is that so? Well, Lord Wolverton *was* hailed as a war hero in all the papers."

Christian scowled at her, and Alice could hardly refrain from laughing at the sight. "It was nothing, really." He approached the bench opposite the one Alice was sitting on with Pembroke, and helped Miss Beasley before taking a seat himself. "How are you enjoying the day, Lady Alice?"

His eyes captured hers and were focused and intense. It was as if he were silently interviewing her with just a look. "It's a fine day. I especially have enjoyed the conversation."

Pembroke looked over at her with a small smile, but her eyes were drawn back to Christian's. "But I really should go soon in case my help is needed for our *al fresco* repast. My mother decided to have the picnic set up at the old abbey ruins on the east side of the estate." She leaned toward Miss Beasley. "The ruins are said to be haunted, you know."

Miss Beasley's eyes widened. "Are you sure it's safe for ladies?"

Alice waved a hand. "With Lord Wolverton at your side, you have no cause to fret. He'll protect you." This time Christian was able to stifle a scowl, but he clenched his jaw so hard it was a wonder he didn't break a tooth. Alice couldn't suppress her grin. "We're all so lucky to have him in our midst."

"Aren't you doing it a bit brown, my lady?" Christian could barely paste his society smile on.

"Not at all." She gave him her most wide-eyed, innocent look. "But I'm afraid I must hurry back in case my mother needs my assistance." Normally, the duchess was quite organized and prepared, but since Lady Elizabeth had to bow out of the party so suddenly, the numbers were uneven and her mother had been in a dither all morning. Alice might very well be the calming influence she needed.

"But I was hoping we could stay a little longer and finish our conversation." Lord Pembroke kept his voice low, though there was no doubt Christian and Miss Beasley could easily hear him.

"And I wanted to stay and enjoy the folly as well," Miss Beasley put in, her lips forming a little pout for Christian's benefit.

"Oh, how perfect." Alice clapped her hands together. "Lord Pembroke, you can stay with Miss Beasley at the folly, so she doesn't miss out on any of the afternoon's entertainments. Lord Wolverton can row me to shore and escort me to the abbey ruins.

We'll have plenty of time to finish our conversation when you join us."

Pembroke started to protest, but Christian immediately stood up. "As you wish, my lady." He offered his hand to help her stand, which Alice immediately took.

"Thank you for your assistance, my lord." She took his arm and turned back to Pembroke. "And for yours."

They took their leave and started to move up the path. Christian didn't say anything at all, as Alice knew he wouldn't, not until they were out of Pembroke's hearing. As they made their way to the boats, he bent his head toward her. "Have you changed your opinions about his innocence?"

"Not at all. He confessed to me that his final conversation with Thomas was about an investment they were both involved in, not anything sinister at all. Oh!" She stumbled on the path and Christian caught her, sweeping her to his side and holding her there.

"Is your ankle paining you?" His eyes searched hers, wanting the truth.

She closed her eyes and indulged herself by inhaling his familiar scent before she opened them. "A little. But it's nothing."

"You ought to be home in bed." He shook his head. "But I understand why you are out here. Digging for the truth, protecting the Crown. It's more of a calling than a choice, isn't it?"

Alice's mouth fell open. No one had ever articulated what she felt in her heart so clearly. "Exactly."

Christian touched her shoulder. "Would it help if I carried you to the boat? You should probably sit as much as possible."

Her heart fluttered a bit at the thought of him holding her. She had felt quite safe in his arms when he'd carried her to the horse last night. But she couldn't be distracted by his closeness. "I'm fine. If we could just slow our pace."

He agreed and took her arm once again. She leaned on him, and it did feel good to have that support. "I know you are convinced of Pembroke's guilt, but once he confessed the whole of his association with Thomas, I am more convinced that he is innocent."

"Since it is widely known their conversation was angry and intense, it is only reasonable to suspect that their investment didn't go well." Christian spoke slowly, as if he was making connections in his mind.

Alice's stomach twisted. "The ship was lost at sea and the cargo sank with it. But Pembroke assured me that Thomas was alive and hiring a hackney when he left. He showed no signs of telling a falsehood through his breathing, tone, or eye movement."

"Anyone who betrays his country will be an accomplished liar. And the failed investment gives him a motive for killing, as well as a motive for selling the names of the agents. He must be desperate for funds." Christian slowed his pace even more. "Do you want him to be innocent because you've developed an affection for him?"

His voice was steady, though his eyes were unreadable. Alice shook her head. "I don't have to have a *tendre* for someone to want their name cleared if they are innocent."

"Ah, but that very thing could cloud your judgment." He sounded so sure of himself. It was maddening. Why did men think that a woman couldn't be in an eligible gentleman's company without losing her head? Thankfully, they had arrived at the boat, and her need for his support had come to an end.

"You have no need to worry, my lord. I am well aware of how to do my job." Alice carefully moved past him and seated herself in the boat.

What she needed was solid evidence to bring to Christian and her father to prove Lord Pembroke's innocence once and for all. And to do that, she would have to search his rooms.

But time was running out. She'd have to do it tonight.

CHAPTER 10

Christian watched Alice leave the dining room and adjourn to the parlor with the other women. She was listening intently to something Miss Beasley was saying, her hair swept up with little curls framing her face. She was smiling, and her cheeks were pink. He couldn't stop thinking of how good she'd felt at his side when he'd escorted her to the boat, supporting her so she didn't put much weight on her injured ankle.

She fit so well against him. Her show of pique when he'd pressed to know about her feelings for Pembroke had reassured him somewhat, though it was possible her judgment could still possibly be obscured by Pembroke's attempts to dazzle her. That was why he needed to search Pembroke's rooms tonight. Alice was so sure of his innocence, and Christian was just as sure of his guilt. Tonight, he was going to prove it one way or the other.

Pulling his gaze away as the door shut behind her, he went to stand next to the duke. After he'd accepted a glass of port from the footman, he took a small sip. He was going to need his wits about him tonight. The duke acknowledged him, but didn't stop his conversation with the vicar about attending Sunday services. The duke wore the same expression Alice had, listening intently to the person they were with as if there wasn't anyone else in the room. Yet, with the duke's reputation for attention to detail, he had no doubt Alice had also been trained in being aware of everyone around them. Fascinated, Christian watched the duke's fingers tighten on his drink as his glance flicked toward a man approaching him.

Pembroke.

"Your Grace, may I have a private audience with you? I have a matter of importance I'd like to discuss." Pembroke was clutching his tumbler as if it were a life preserver, but his eyes were wide and hopeful, like an eager hound dog expecting a bone.

"What is it concerning?" the duke asked carefully, sipping his drink and taking Pembroke's measure with a practiced stare.

Pembroke visibly swallowed. "Your Grace, it's concerning your daughter."

The room quieted as the men around them moved closer at the sudden tension in the air. The duke glanced at them, then put his drink on a tray. "Let's take this conversation to my study."

An iron band seemed to be squeezing the air out of Christian's lungs. Pembroke having an audience with the duke about Alice was wrong, all wrong. There was no doubt he would ask for permission to formally court her. With the charges being leveled against Pembroke, the duke would likely decline, but Christian couldn't be sure. Alice was convinced of Pembroke's innocence. Did the duke share her opinion?

His hand clenched and unclenched. He had to focus. No matter what Pembroke was planning for Alice, he would be occupied in the duke's study for a time. This was Christian's chance to search Pembroke's rooms. Getting evidence against him was more important then ever.

Christian ground his teeth and deliberately spilled port on his cravat. "Oh, bother," he said to Lord Stafford and the vicar, who were still standing nearby. "Excuse me a moment while I go change. It wouldn't do to have a stain for the evening entertainment."

The men agreed and Christian took his leave. Quietly opening the door the duke and Pembroke had just passed through, he walked down the hallway toward the guest wing. Christian looked at the closed parlor door, where he could hear a murmur of higher-pitched voices and laughter. Had Alice thought of him this evening? Shaking his head, he sternly put away all thoughts of Alice and turned the corner toward the staircase. He should be thinking of Pembroke's rooms and devising a search plan. He wouldn't have much time.

As he walked down the hall with the eyes of the Huntingdon ancestors staring at him from their portraits and moved toward the central marble staircase, a sense of belonging washed over him that he hadn't felt in a long time. He'd had plenty of experience being in situations where he didn't belong. Like the time he'd spied on enemy troop movements when a French scout had caught him by surprise. Christian had been hustled back to the scout's superior. Luckily, he hadn't been in uniform. His stained and torn clothing had helped convince the man that Christian was merely an impoverished Spanish farmer who was too afraid to speak. The little Spanish he knew had solidified his ruse, and they'd let him go.

Tonight, however, he was a marquess in a duke's home. He belonged. If he was discovered searching a gentleman's room, he could say he had business with Pembroke and was merely looking for him. Still, adrenaline pumped through his veins as he climbed the staircase, like a familiar friend he'd thought he left in Spain, but had suddenly joined him again.

Putting on the mantle of a marquess that he'd learned from his father and brother— both powerful men that no one had dared to trifle with— he strode down the hall to the wing where the guest rooms were, passing his own bedchamber. Pembroke's was only four doors down. As Christian got closer, however, he noted the lamps near Pembroke's door were out. Something was wrong. Christian stopped and cautiously moved forward, his senses on alert. Pembroke's door swung open, and his valet stepped into the hall, startling him. Christian quickly moved back to his own door, as if he were about to go in.

He turned and met the valet's gaze, but the man deferentially ducked his head. "My lord."

Christian acknowledged the gesture with a quick nod, and the man kept walking. The valet didn't look back or seem suspicious as he walked toward the servants' stairs. That had been too close. Christian decided to wait a few moments more before approaching Pembroke's room again. He unlocked his own bedchamber door and walked in. After pacing the length of the small sitting room half a dozen times, he couldn't wait any longer. Pembroke's plea to the duke shouldn't take long. Christian took a deep breath and moved into the corridor, closing his door behind him.

This was his chance.

Walking through the darkened corridor, he stood in front of Pembroke's door and tried the handle. As expected, it was locked. He slipped his lock-picking tools out of his jacket pocket and went to work. He bent close as he manipulated the tumblers until he heard the satisfying click of the lock giving way. After one last look to make sure the hallway was empty, he went inside.

The chamber was nearly identical to his own, with a small sitting area that led into the sleeping chamber and dressing room. A low fire was burning in Pembroke's sitting room, though the lamps were lit and the setting sun provided plenty of light. He didn't give the sitting room much thought. If he were planning to betray his country, he wouldn't leave evidence lying about the sitting room. He'd definitely keep such things close in the bedchamber. If there was time, and he hadn't found anything in the bedchamber, he'd come back and search here.

Christian headed for the archway that led to the sleeping area, when the hairs on the back of his neck prickled. He knew that feeling well and had learned to heed it during the war.

Someone was watching him.

Positioning the dagger in his hand, he quickly turned the corner, crouched and ready to pounce.

"Oh!" Alice was in the corner next to the dressing room, in nearly an identical posture, her dagger at the ready. "It's you."

"What are you doing here?" The sight of her in the room, armed, yet calm, sent a sudden awareness through him, as if he'd been struck by a bolt of lightning. She was magnificent. He could hardly tear his gaze away from her bright eyes, flushed cheeks, and her lithe form in a fighting stance.

But she was taking chances with her safety that drove all his protective impulses forward. He took a few extra seconds putting his dagger back into its sheath to gather his thoughts and calm his pounding heart.

"What am I doing here?" She arched a brow. "I'm searching for evidence, which I assume you are doing as well."

Her knife disappeared into the folds of her skirt. Was the sheath attached to her waist? How did she secure it? Christian was curious, but there wasn't time to pursue an answer.

Alice had promptly gone back to searching the room, opening the writing desk drawer in the corner. Christian came up behind her and peered over her shoulder at the contents. "Have you found anything?"

She shook her head, her curls tickling his nose. "Not yet, but I haven't been here long." She bent and opened another drawer.

And she wouldn't be here a moment longer than she had to, if Christian had anything to say about it. "What excuse did you give to take your leave?"

She straightened and held out her skirt with a grin. "A torn flounce. It shouldn't take long to repair."

"Clever. Especially since there isn't much time. If we're not careful, Pembroke could retire early or want a change of clothes before the entertainment begins, and find us here." She was in close proximity again, and Christian couldn't help taking a deep breath. Her rosewater scent was intoxicating.

Steeling himself, he moved away. He'd never had distractions like this on a mission before. He wasn't a green lad who'd never been in the same room with a beautiful woman, but he couldn't stop feeling that way when Alice was near. He had to put distance between them.

"I'll search the trunk near the bed," he said, a little too curt.

Alice barely acknowledged his words with a nod and leaned down to search the very back of the desk drawers with a sweep of her arm. "Fine." She obviously wasn't having any trouble concentrating.

Christian bent to his task, willing to prove that he hadn't lost the skills required to search a room and leave it exactly the way he'd found it. He opened the trunk lid and set aside Pembroke's clothes that had been stored inside, careful not to disturb the order or folds, looking for a false bottom. He didn't find one.

He had to ask her. "What was your plan if Pembroke came back early? It wouldn't do for you to be caught in his bedchamber. Your father would have no choice but to give his consent to the marriage. You'd be ruined." He could hardly bear the thought of her being forced to marry Pembroke. No, he wouldn't allow it to ever come to that. He pushed the beastly thought away.

"I won't be caught. My maid is watching the study and will come and warn me as soon as he leaves." Her tone was so confident and collected. This obviously wasn't her first time searching a room. That small fact fascinated him.

She opened the last drawer and held up a packet of letters.

Turning it toward the light, she read the name of the sender. "He writes his mother regularly."

"He's probably hoping to give her good news after his audience with your father." Christian looked up to see her reaction. Was she anticipating Pembroke's addresses?

"I'm sure he is." She blew a stray hair off of her cheek. "As much as I enjoy our scintillating conversation, perhaps we should focus on dividing the room to search more effectively."

"Of course." Her words felt like he'd jumped into a cold lake. He was an experienced agent acting like this was his first assignment. Pulling his mind to the task at hand, Christian closed the trunk and moved to the bed. His back was to Alice, though no matter what he did, he was still very much aware of her movements.

Lifting the mattress, he looked underneath each corner. Nothing. There wasn't anything underneath the bed, either, though he observed how meticulous the duke's servants were in their work. There wasn't even any dust. Christian was impressed.

Alice moved to the small dressing room next to the fireplace. Christian hadn't found anything in the trunk or mattress, so he joined her. She was already searching Pembroke's jacket pockets, so he started at the other end of the wardrobe and worked toward her. Most of Pembroke's jackets were black, cut with fine material. Some were more worn than others, the buttons dull rather than bright, but all were in good condition. His valet was very good at his job.

When they were through searching all the jacket pockets, all they had to show for their efforts was some loose threads and a few shillings. Perhaps they wouldn't get the evidence they were looking for after all. Alice stooped down to look inside a pair of riding boots, moving them closer to her and revealing a bundle hidden behind them.

"Alice."

She saw it, too, and met his eyes, the air around them suddenly heavy. This was what they'd been looking for. Alice bent down to pick up the cloth that had been tightly knotted at each end. They both worked to undo the careful ties. When the fabric fell away, they both stared at the black clothing inside as if frozen.

Alice was the first to move. She pulled the black fabric into her hands and shook it out. It was a man's shirt. One that was streaked with dirt, with a large bloodstain on the shoulder.

"I believed him," she murmured, staring at the fabric as if willing it to disappear. When she raised her eyes to his, they were stricken.

Christian's heart sank, knowing how it felt to have misplaced one's trust. A hard lesson, to be sure, but necessary for agents. Christian wished he could soften the blow for her.

She pulled the other item from the bundle he still held in his hands. It was a pair of breeches that boasted a torn piece roughly the same shape as the one they found on the bush this morning. Her lips formed a thin line. "I made excuses for him. When he told me his story, he gave every indication he was telling the truth." She crumpled the clothing into a ball and shoved it back into the bundle. "He's a very good liar."

Christian retied the knots, watching the play of frustration and anger flit across her face. "I know this is difficult, and that you're feeling betrayed, but we can't confront him. Not yet. We must catch the French buyer."

She folded her arms, staring at the bundle in his hand as if he held a snake. "We have our proof now. You were right all along." Her voice was flat and unemotional, though he knew a riot of emotions simmered just below the surface.

Looking at her face, Christian didn't want to be right. Curse Pembroke and his greedy, traitorous ways. He set the bundle back exactly where they'd found it and then reached for her, cupping her shoulders. "Now that we have evidence against him, we can make sure he pays for his crimes."

Her small fists clenched, and she rested them on his chest. "He won't get away with this. Tomorrow can't come soon enough."

"We have to rejoin the others before we're discovered." Though he would rather have stayed with Alice and talked through their suspicions in light of what they'd found, lingering in Pembroke's dressing room could end in disaster.

"Yes, we should go." She looked up at him with a little jog of her chin and squared her shoulders. "We have some planning to do and not a moment to lose.

Christian squeezed her arms and stepped back so she could precede him out of the dressing room. Her illusions were broken, but with her jaw set and the determined look on her face, Pembroke didn't stand a chance.

And Christian didn't want to miss a moment of Alice giving Pembroke the comeuppance he deserved.

CHAPTER 11

The duchess stood the moment Alice entered the music room. "Oh there you are, my dear. We didn't want to start without you. Lord Pembroke was just telling me how he's looking forward to hearing you play."

Alice lowered her eyes, not wanting her mother to see the flash of anger at the mention of Pembroke's name. "I'm certain that Lord Pembroke was just being kind."

A fire burned cheerfully on one end of the room, with the pianoforte in the middle. She'd always loved this room with its large windows that let the light shine in. Tonight, though, the sun had set, and it was dark outside— just how Alice felt on the inside after her discovery in Pembroke's dressing room.

She sat down on a small, upholstered chair near her mother. Pembroke was only two seats to her left, sitting with Penelope Beasley. He gave her an enthusiastic smile, and she ground her teeth. It was all she could do to keep her seat and not stand and confront him with what she knew. But Alice drew on her years of comportment lessons and training for her role in the Falcon Group and calmly stayed where she was.

Her gaze kept returning to him as they waited for Penelope and Beatrice to finish looking through the music and decide which pieces to play. Alice folded her hands in her lap, trying to control her temper and not appear disagreeable. How could she have been so wrong about Pembroke? He'd given such a convincing performance he could have a career on Drury Lane. But he'd obviously become complacent by leaving that bundle of clothing in his room. She turned away and took a deep breath. She would remain quiet tonight for Thomas's sake. Because once Pembroke was caught in the act of treason, Thomas would have justice.

Shaking off her thoughts, she faced forward to listen to Penelope on the pianoforte. She'd chosen an early, less-complicated piece by Mozart that showed her talent in its best light. When she was through, the audience clapped in a lively manner to show their appreciation. Penelope blushed as she made her curtsy and returned to her seat.

"Alice?" the duchess said, opening her fan. "What will you grace us with this evening?"

"I've decided on one of my favorites." Alice moved to the bench at the pianoforte that Penelope had just vacated and sat down. She didn't need any music for the arrangement. Whenever she needed a way to release pent-up frustration, she played the "Presto Agitato" movement from her favorite Beethoven concerto. It fit her mood perfectly tonight.

Out of the corner of her eye she could see Pembroke beaming at her. Christian was near the doorway, almost in the shadows, but she could feel his eyes on her. The turmoil inside her built as everything she'd experienced over the past few days bubbled to the surface. She focused on the piano keys.

The agitation she'd been feeling flowed through her fingers and into the music. The chords were heavy, echoing through her wrists, her arms, her body. The arpeggios were her chance for her fingers to fly and match her galloping thoughts. Images flashed through her mind as she played: the gunshot at the ball, the attack last night, the bundle in the closet.

Christian.

His eyes that saw her soul. His arms that offered comfort. He stirred feelings in her she'd never thought possible. What was she to do?

When her fingers pressed down for the last chord, she closed her eyes to feel the notes lift into the air and take some of her tension with them. As the sound faded, she opened her eyes and took a deep breath, feeling lighter. She always did when she played that particular piece. The room was silent for a moment before the audience began to applaud. Everyone stood, and some even called for an encore. Dipping into a low curtsy, she rose.

"Thank you," she said, and moved toward her seat next to her mother. Her eyes sought Christian, who was still standing exactly where he'd been when she started. His arms were folded, though his gaze was full of warmth that she felt to the tips of her toes.

But like a rush of cold wind, the warmth fled when Pembroke appeared in front of her. He held out a hand, and for just a second, Alice considered snubbing him. *For Thomas,* she reminded herself. *Be polite for him.*

Pembroke took her offered hand and bowed low, then kissed her knuckles. "Brilliant, my lady. Simply brilliant."

Every eye in the room was on them, and Alice was annoyed he was making such a spectacle. But she smiled and murmured her thanks, though the words almost stuck in her throat. Acting as if nothing was wrong was becoming more difficult by the moment.

Pembroke retreated, and once everyone was seated again, Penelope and Lady Beatrice sang for the assembled guests, their pure voices washing over Alice until she was lost in the beauty of them. Lord Stafford, a house guest who had been mostly quiet the entire time he'd been in company, stood to sing an Irish air, surprising them all with his deep, rich baritone. When the last note floated away and the applause had died down, the duchess stood.

"Thank you all for a wonderful evening." The duchess looked over the group, who had stood with her. "The gentlemen must be ready at the break of dawn for the hunt in the morning, so I won't hold them here any longer." She smiled at her guests. "And of course, we ladies will be readying ourselves for the masquerade tomorrow evening."

Penelope giggled and started to move to the duchess to wish her goodnight. Alice was at her mother's side and received several compliments for her contribution to the musical program. Her cheeks were starting to ache from the smile she'd pasted on her face. She needed to escape, not only to relieve her sore cheeks, but before Pembroke could approach. Just as she was about to take her leave, her father appeared at her side.

"Alice, I hate to spirit you away, but will you join me in my study for a moment?" the duke asked, smiling down at her.

"Of course." Alice took his elbow, glad he had sought her out and saved her from another encounter with Pembroke.

They walked slowly down the corridor that led to his study, the lamps casting shadows across the floor. "You played magnificently tonight," her father said, giving her a side glance. "Though I do remember your penchant for playing that song when you are particularly out of sorts."

She ducked her head. "Am I so obvious?" She sighed. "Once I tell you what's happened, you will understand the cause."

He didn't press her further. When he opened the door to his study, the familiar scent of leather and old books washed over her, reminding her of all the time she'd spent in here as a child, reading when he was doing estate business, or discussing how her lessons were coming, or what her plans were for the day. This room had been the center of her memories with her father, and it was comforting. Some more of the tension she'd been feeling drained away.

She sat in the armchair directly across from her father's desk—the one she thought of as hers. Before the interview with her father proceeded, however, Christian appeared in the open doorway.

"Your Grace, Lady Alice," he said, sketching a bow before he sat in the chair next to hers.

"Wolverton." The duke acknowledged him with a tilt of his head before he closed the door. "It seems as if there's been a development."

He walked behind his desk and sat down, his eyes resting on Alice. "You mentioned that something has happened. Does this development confirm your theory that Pembroke is innocent? When he met with me this evening, he did inform me that his earldom is deep in debt and he had counted on the investment partnership with Thomas to help him save his family's seat. He also reassured me several times that Thomas was alive when he left him outside of White's."

"He told me the same thing." Alice twisted her hands together in her lap, then stilled them. She had to stay in control. Analyze the information objectively.

"He was quite earnest when he told me the story." The duke stroked his chin and glanced at Christian. "Though I did note the amount of money that the list of agents is being sold for is nearly the exact amount Lord Pembroke needs to settle his debts."

Alice leaned forward, her frustration bubbling to the surface once again. "All my instincts told me he was innocent, but the evidence keeps mounting against him." She held up a finger. "Pembroke confessed he'd hurt his right arm, which likely means he is the man I stabbed last night." She held up a second finger. "His debts would be settled with the sale of the list. And when we searched his rooms earlier— " she held up a third finger, "we found a bundle of dirty, black clothing with blood on it, which surely belongs to my attacker."

The duke didn't react right away. He shifted in his chair, looking between Alice and Christian. "The strange thing is that during our meeting he talked of needing Alice's dowry to restore the earldom, though he assured me of his regard for you, my dear. Why would he tell me of his need for your dowry if he would have the money from the sale? Your instincts are rarely ever wrong, Alice. Perhaps, this time, we're reaching our conclusions too quickly."

Christian cleared his throat. "The clothing in his dressing room matches the fabric we found in the wood this morning. He admits he needs money, and he has contacts in the peerage and Foreign Office that could have given him access to the names on the list. All leads point to Pembroke and his guilt. And with all the investigations that have been performed, there are no other suspects that I'm aware of here, nor any other noblemen that have been spotted in Kent, except those that are here."

The duke steepled his fingers again. "I'm merely trying to see all the angles. Something doesn't feel right." He was quiet for a moment. "We must be prepared for all contingencies, both if he is innocent or if he is truly guilty. Regardless, the exchange will take place tomorrow, and Pembroke will be watched carefully. I've got extra footmen in place, a dozen agents on the ground, and every guest has been given a thorough check of their recent activities."

Christian sat up straighter in his chair, the leather creaking with the movement. "Your Grace, I must ask, has the investigation into Viscount Carlisle been reported? Does he fit into Pembroke's scheme?"

Alice remembered the viscount from the night of the ball where she'd first met Christian. She hadn't noticed a strong connection between the two men that night. Could they be friends rather than just acquaintances?

"I had him thoroughly scrutinized, and he's not party to Pembroke's scheme. Carlisle is in the devil's own scrape, though. He's buying up Pembroke's gambling vowels so he'll be beholden to him. From the information we have, Carlisle is trying to break his betrothal with Pembroke's sister." The duke drummed his fingers on the table.

Christian frowned. "Carlisle is betrothed to Pembroke's sister?"

"Not for much longer, if Carlisle has his way," the duke said with a shake of his head. "The man has had some demons in him ever since he returned from the war. I'm surprised the lady in question doesn't want to cry off herself with the way the viscount has been comporting himself."

"He's still trying to numb his memories of the war, I'll wager. But indulging in liquor isn't a treasonous act." Relief mixed with concern colored Christian's tone.

"Did you know the viscount well?" Alice asked, wanting to know more.

"Only as his superior officer," Christian said, turning toward her. "He saw some of the worst of humanity. We all did. I'm afraid he's not dealing with it well, and I was concerned he'd turned his anger and bitterness against the country he'd defended. I'm glad he hasn't."

"I am, too." Facing a friend's betrayal was a difficult, inner pain to deal with. Though Alice hadn't counted Pembroke as a friend, really, she had thought well of him and his treachery stung.

"Even with our suspicions about Pembroke, I want you both to be vigilant at the masquerade. Desperation can turn men into monsters." The duke stood and came around to the side of his desk. "Hopefully this situation will be well in hand tomorrow night."

"Yes, Papa." Alice stood as well. Christian stepped to her side and held out his arm to escort her toward the door. She curled her hand around his elbow as if it were the most natural thing in the world. As if she belonged there with him at her side.

"I'll see you for the hunt tomorrow morning," the duke said as he opened the door and walked into the corridor. Alice and Christian followed. "It should be a fine day for shooting."

"I'm assuming the hunting party won't have you for a guide? Or that you have a hidden shooting talent?" Christian looked down at her, a twinkle of amusement in his eyes.

"You can never be sure of my hidden talents, my lord," Alice said with a superior grin. "But I'm afraid I won't be joining the hunting party as a guide, though that will be of no consequence when a legendary tracker like yourself will be in the company." Christian chuckled at her rejoinder. Alice let go of his arm to start for the stairs. "I will bid you goodnight, Lord Wolverton. Papa."

Before her slipper touched the carpet of the first stair, a footman approached, Christian and bowed. "A note for you, Lord Wolverton."

Alice froze, her hand on the railing. Her father received notes and visitors at all hours during an active mission. But who would send a note this late to Christian unless it was regarding Lord Pembroke?

Her father paused as well. "Inform me of any developments," he said, his voice low, but filled with authority. Christian had nodded toward the duke before he broke the seal. Alice wanted to stay and see what the note said, but her father offered his arm. "Shall I escort you to your room, Alice?"

"Of course." She resisted the urge to look back as they climbed the staircase, but she knew Christian was still standing where they'd left him. Had it been bad news? When they reached the door to her bedchamber, she gave her father a kiss on the cheek. "Thank you, Papa." She turned to go inside, but he put his hand on her forearm.

"I know this case has been difficult for you, and it's not over yet. I'm not convinced Pembroke is the traitor, and there have already been two attempts on your life. Please be careful tomorrow. Use an escort. Make sure you are armed and have an escort with you where possible." Her father's kind, yet worried, eyes rested on her.

She kissed his cheek once again. "You've taught me well, Papa. Don't worry."

He smiled and squeezed her shoulder. "I'm very proud of you and all that you've accomplished. So is your mother."

Tears rose suddenly and stung the back of her throat. Her father loved her, she'd always known that, but to have earned his pride meant everything. "I had a wonderful teacher."

He smiled and let her go. She slipped inside her room, basking in the glow of her father's love for just a moment— and giving him time to reach his own rooms. Keeping an ear to her door, she listened to her father's fading footsteps, counted to one hundred, then moved back into the corridor and crept downstairs. She had to talk to Christian and find out what was in that note.

Alice hoped he hadn't gone to his room. No matter how badly she wanted to know what the message said, she couldn't risk her reputation by going alone to a man's bedchamber at night. When she got downstairs, however, Christian wasn't to be found. She checked the parlor, library, music room, and billiards room. Heaving a sigh, Alice faced the fact that she would likely have to wait until tomorrow to know the contents of the note.

Her stomach rumbled, and Alice recalled she'd merely picked at her dinner, trying to keep up polite conversation and devise a way to search Pembroke's rooms without being caught. Deciding to see if Cook had any bread and jam or honey cake left in the kitchen, she headed down there. As she opened the door, she heard the rumble of voices. Christian and a stable hand were sitting at the table.

When he saw her, Christian rose immediately, his chair

scraping loudly across the floor. "Alice, I thought you'd gone to bed."

She smiled, relieved to have found him. Moving toward the pair, she stood next to the small table. "I couldn't sleep for wondering what was in the note you received. May I sit down?"

"I should have known that someone with your curiosity would never be able to rest for not knowing what was in a note." Christian grinned and held the chair to his right for her. "Lady Alice, may I present to you Lieutenant Colin Pearce."

Pearce dipped his head out of respect. "Forgive me for not rising, my lady. My wound isn't quite healed."

"Lieutenant?" She glanced at Christian. "Did you serve with Lord Wolverton then?"

"Proudly." Pearce inclined his head toward Christian. "There wasn't a better commander on the field."

She lowered her voice, but Cook's snoring that was coming from her room would have covered any noise. "And now you work for the Falcon Group." Alice remembered Christian mentioning it once. "You were the stable hand that was stabbed yesterday." The pieces were fitting together. He was one of the men her father had called in and the one who had chased the intruder. Alice had wanted to question him earlier, but he'd been drugged with laudanum.

"Yes. It's a good thing I'm tough as leather," Pearce said, puffing out his chest, then wincing. "Happened so fast I didn't have a chance to take my own knife out of my boot."

Alice leaned forward, clasping her hands on the table. "Did you see the intruder? Could you identify him?"

Pearce shook his head. "It was dark, and he was wearing a black stocking cap with some blonde hair sticking out the end. He was a large chap, though, with a longish nose."

Blonde hair. Long nose. Pembroke. Alice looked at Christian, who stared back at her with a solemn expression. Yesterday she would have suggested that any number of men could have fit that description. But with the bundle of clothes, coupled with the amount of money from the sale being exactly what Pembroke needed, it didn't seem like coincidence. The money had just been one more piece of evidence against him, and now they had Pearce's witness to add to it.

"That is nearly the same description I got from the witness who saw the man that killed Thomas." Christian grimaced, his fingers curling into a fist on the table. "And he nearly killed you, Pearce. After all the battles you survived in Spain, I could hardly bear the thought of you dying at home, on English soil."

Pearce coughed and held his side. "I've still got a few good years left in me, I suppose." He stood slowly, leaning heavily on a cane. "I'm sorry I don't have more information, but we'll all be watching for anyone who doesn't belong here, and we'll help in any way we can."

Alice watched as Christian got up to help Pearce to the servants' entrance so he could return to the stables. His normal military posture was bent over to provide support for Pearce. Sometimes he seemed every inch the marquess he was—arrogant and sure of himself— but he'd constantly showed her that he cared for people, whether servants or friends. He was concerned for Viscount Carlisle and even now was helping an old friend to the door. Christian had shown tenderness to her as well after she'd been attacked, and then again this afternoon when he'd helped her to the boat. He was a complicated man, and he hid a caring heart.

Christian rejoined her at the table, and she was suddenly very aware that they were alone in a darkened kitchen with only a candle between them. "He was very lucky he wasn't killed," she said, glad her voice didn't betray her warm thoughts of the man sitting across the small table from her.

Christian leaned forward, closing the distance, and her heart skipped a beat at his nearness. His eyes were fathomless in the dim light, but she could feel the intensity of his gaze. He reached out and took her hand, letting his thumb skim over the back, his touch heating her skin like a stoked fire on a cold day. "I want you to be very careful tomorrow. Heed your father's words. Desperation can make men into monsters. Don't take any chances at all."

His touch sparked tingles through her hand and up her arm, as if a fire was spreading through her body. How could one man affect her so? "And you as well. This is a dangerous game Pembroke is playing."

She couldn't look away from him, the candlelight and shadows drawing a curtain around them until it was as if they were the only two people in the world. His hair looked like burnished bronze, and her fingers itched to touch it. Was it as soft as it looked?

"I know tonight was difficult for you, finding out about Pembroke's guilt, but you can't be anything other than amiable to him, or he'll know something is amiss and bolt." Christian gently touched her cheek. "Much as I hate the idea of you being near him at all."

"Christian," she started, her voice quiet, savoring his given name on her lips. "I wonder . . . Well, as part of your circle, I need to ask you something. Did you ever have nerves before a coming battle? I know what's expected tomorrow with the list and Pembroke, but part of me is frightened that it won't go as planned. That we might lose the list and what repercussions there would be if we did."

His fingers tightened around hers as he contemplated his answer. "Much as I wish I could say I didn't feel afraid and nervous before a battle, the answer is yes. Thinking about what was to come, feeling the dread around us like an intruder who stole conversation, jokes, and hope. We'd all sit at the fire, writing letters that we hoped weren't our last, talking of home, saying a prayer in case we met our Maker the next day. But we all embraced one other before we retired with a hearty slap on the back and a 'In victory or defeat, we stand together.'" He reached out to cup her face, and she leaned her cheek into his palm. "There will be no defeat for us tomorrow. I promise you that."

She wanted to believe him, to seal that promise as a vow. Closing the small distance between them, she brushed her lips with his. "Thank you," she whispered.

He gently tugged her back to him and pressed his lips more firmly to hers. Her heart raced as his kiss deepened and everything else faded away. There weren't any other feelings to sort out as long as his mouth moved over hers. Her hand reached up to his face, feeling the stubble there as her fingers traced his jaw. She closed her eyes, her heartbeat pounding his name through her veins. *Christian. Christian.* She savored the kiss, but the timing wasn't right. Not yet. Reluctantly, she drew away.

"Alice?" he started, but she put her fingers to his lips.

She rose from the table, wanting to kiss him again, but knowing she shouldn't. If she did, she wouldn't want to stop. Her feelings for Christian were complicated and confusing, tangled up in their work to build a case against Pembroke. She needed more time to think and not to have a threat of danger hovering over them. "Tomorrow we'll stand together. In victory. Then perhaps we can continue this . . . conversation."

A corner of his lips curved into a half smile as he moved to stand in front of her. His thumb traced an invisible trail down her cheek to her jaw. The embers of need flared between them again, and Alice's feet were rooted to the floor. She wanted his arms to come around her, to feel his kiss on her lips, his hands in her hair. No man had ever affected her thus, and it was a heady feeling.

His eyes were dark and shadowed as he looked at her, his breaths shallow. Alice's heart thrilled at the thought that he wanted the same thing she did.

But he stepped back, breaking the spell around them. "Until

tomorrow then," he said, his voice hardly more than a low growl in his throat.

"Until tomorrow," she whispered, not trusting herself to speak out loud. She let her fingers linger on the lapel of his coat for just a moment longer before she turned and walked from the room.

A chill enveloped her as soon as she left Christian in the cozy kitchen. Touching her lips, she walked upstairs, unable to keep the smile from her face. She couldn't wait for tomorrow to be over and to have the list safe. Then, maybe she could explore the connection she had with Christian and see if they could suit as more than partners in espionage.

CHAPTER 12

The morning boasted a fine drizzle of rain that tapered
off as the men all gathered on the east lawn, their
mounts anxious to start the shoot as the dogs danced around the
horses' feet. How many times had Christian and his brother John
joined their father to hunt on just such a morning? Being home in
England had brought all sorts of memories to the fore, some good
and some that hurt to think about. Everything was different now.
Christian pulled his greatcoat closer around him, wishing he were
still in his warm bed with a cheery fire going in the hearth. He'd
spent too many nights on the cold ground in Spain, and his body
craved the comforts he'd taken for granted before the war.

Soon enough, the duke led the shooting party into the woods.
Christian watched the men ride off, but Pembroke hung at the
back of the group. Maneuvering nearer to him, Christian gave
himself the task of staying close to Pembroke in case he was planning another attempt on an agent's life. Christian didn't recognize
all the operatives the duke had summoned to the house, of course,
but anyone with the list would know who to target. But perhaps

Pembroke would think twice about any further attempts if Christian was close by.

Pembroke didn't look pleased at Christian's proximity, but he didn't say anything as they rode on. When the horses slowed to a canter, and the other men had drawn far ahead of them, Christian decided to open up the conversation. "Have you known Edward Carlisle long?"

Pembroke gave him a sidelong glance, as if surprised Christian was speaking to him. "Our family estates are next to each other. We grew up together."

That explained the betrothal between Pembroke's sister and Carlisle. "Did you get a chance to sort out the business you two were discussing at the ball?" Perhaps if Christian pressed, Pembroke would reveal something he wasn't planning on sharing and give a clue as to when the exchange with the French buyer would take place.

"No, not really. Edward is a changed man since he's returned from war. It's very difficult to find a time when he's sober enough to discuss business." Pembroke adjusted the reins in his hand. "But I am determined to try again when I return to London."

Christian moved a tree branch aside so he could pass under it. They would soon be at the appointed place to wait for the game-keeper's men to flush the game birds out to the men waiting with their rifles. Then his chance to speak with Pembroke would be over. "Perhaps I can help," he offered.

"I don't see how you could. Edward doesn't listen to anyone these days." He looked down, letting out a great sigh, his chin dipping. "And I've made matters worse by giving him a weapon to hold over me."

Christian straightened in the saddle. Did he mean the gambling vowels? Or had he told Edward about the list? "What weapon is that?"

"It's a family matter, I'm afraid. But once I return to London, I'll be able to make it right." Pembroke clenched his jaw and looked straight ahead, the tension flowing from him. "I feel I must be direct, Lord Wolverton, since you have sought me out this morning. I'm working to secure the affections of Lady Alice, and I have felt in recent days that you are perhaps my rival in that endeavor. But I assure you, I will soon be taking the next step of securing her hand in marriage, now that I have received her father's permission to court her." He stared at Christian, obviously staking his claim to the lady.

Christian furrowed his brow as Pembroke's words sank in. If the goal was to dismantle the Falcon Group, and he knew Lady Alice was a member of it, why would he court her? If Pembroke's demeanor was any indication, he truly saw Christian as a rival. A niggling doubt started to form in the back of his mind. Had they been too hasty in believing Pembroke guilty? Or was Pembroke a master manipulator?

Either way, he didn't want him courting Alice. Christian leaned back in the saddle and met the earl's gaze. "Do you have Lady Alice's permission as well?" After their kiss in the kitchen last night, Christian had thought of little else. Yet, even imagining Pembroke bringing her flowers or speaking with her alone was out of the question. Christian wasn't sure what was between him and Alice, but he wanted the chance to find out.

"I plan to speak with her at the masquerade this evening," Pembroke told him brusquely. "And I expect to have happy news to share very soon."

"You're that sure of her regard?" Christian was curious. If Pembroke was planning on revealing the Duke of Huntingdon's role in the Falcon Group as well as Alice's, how could he expect to marry her? Something wasn't right.

Pembroke slowed his mount to come alongside Christian's. "Lady Alice has heard some distressing rumors about me that aren't true. She has stayed by my side and believed the truth as I told it to her. That kind of loyalty is hard to find, and I don't plan to let her get away. A loyal wife makes for a happy life."

Alice was loyal. Christian silently agreed on that. Clever. Kind. He could think of a long list of words to describe her, but it was one he didn't care to share with Pembroke. "And have you shared these rumors with her father?"

Pembroke looked at him with disdain. "Come, come, Lord Wolverton. Don't pretend you haven't heard the rumor that I killed Thomas Norwich. Half the *ton* is whispering about it— and have been since the day his body was recovered. The duke is well aware of the situation I find myself in."

They were nearing the field where the other men were already forming a line in preparation for shooting the birds. Their conversation would soon have to turn to more polite topics, but Christian wanted an answer. *"Did* you kill him?"

"Of course not. An investment I made fell through, and I was angry with Thomas, but not enough to kill him. I left him alive and went home to finish off a bottle of brandy. The next day I was accused of killing him." Pembroke shook his head, his grip on the reins so tight his knuckles were white. "I liked Thomas."

His last claim was said with so much sadness, not even an accomplished actor could have feigned it. Christian now saw why Alice believed in Pembroke's innocence. He was starting to question his own beliefs about the man's guilt. But what else explained the evidence they'd already gathered?

"I'm sure being accused was very difficult," Christian said, trying to look at the situation from Pembroke's perspective. A failed investment, followed by an allegation of murder, were enough to crush any man if he was innocent. But Pembroke had the access and means to put together a list of agents, and the payoff would solve all of his problems. Had he succumbed to the temptation? Evidence indicated he did, but Pembroke's demeanor suggested otherwise.

After ducking under more trees to try and catch up to the rest of the party, Pembroke let out a puff of air. "It's been extremely hard for my mother and sister." His jaw hardened. "The tabbies of the *ton* are ruthless."

Christian agreed. Since he'd entered society as a young man, he'd seen whispers and rumors ruin a reputation all too often. "But you're confident you can make things right by marrying Lady Alice?"

"With a connection to the Duke of Huntingdon, no one would dare give us the cut direct." Pembroke looked over at Christian. "And she would be happy, I assure you."

Christian doubted someone like Alice, who had so much spirit and passion, could ever be happy in a marriage where she was valued only for her loyalty and connections. She needed someone who would celebrate her unique talents in serving her king and country and who would love her for the vibrant woman she was. *Someone like me.*

The thought came so unbidden that he hardly had time to consider it more thoroughly before he heard himself say, "I'll not be stepping aside. I, too, believe I can make Lady Alice happy."

Pembroke frowned. They were within listening distance of the other men now, and their conversation was nearly at an end. "I was hoping it wouldn't come to this, that you would withdraw your suit when you realized how serious my intentions were."

Christian shrugged. Now that he'd spoken his feelings for Alice, it was as if his course of action had crystallized. She was his match. "While I was in Spain, I never shied away from battle, and I won't in England, either." He cocked his eyebrow and gave Pembroke an icy stare. "And Lady Alice is worth fighting for."

"She has sought out my company during the entire house party. Seeing as her feelings are so obviously engaged, I don't think I shall have any trouble securing her hand. But we shall see who the lady chooses." Pembroke barely gave him a nod as a by-your-leave before he nudged his horse forward to join the other gentlemen.

Christian watched him go. Alice had sought out Pembroke's company for the sake of the investigation, but he'd wondered several times if she'd developed a *tendre* for the man. She'd certainly been affected when they'd found the bundle of clothing in Pembroke's dressing room and she'd held the evidence of his guilt in her hand. Of course, Christian had also spent quite a bit of time with Alice to ferret out the traitor. Last night in the kitchen, she'd said they'd continue the conversation when the traitor had been caught. What kind of conversation did she mean, exactly?

Christian wasn't used to feeling so unsure. The masquerade promised to reveal the traitor's name and, hopefully, his buyer's. But would it also reveal Alice's feelings for him? If he did pursue her, would he have a chance of standing with her at his side?

Since coming home from the war, Christian had felt adrift, trying to make sense of a world that was in chaos. He'd felt needed on the battlefield and working for the Falcon Group. He hadn't wanted to take over his brother's or his father's positions, but that was exactly what was going to happen, and there wasn't anything he could do to change the circumstances. Furthering his acquaintance with Alice had provided an anchor for him that he hadn't known he needed and he didn't want to give her up if there was any chance for him as her suitor.

Dismounting, Christian handed his horse's reins to the waiting groom and turned his thoughts to the task at hand. He took his place on the end of the line of gentleman who laughed and conversed as they waited. He let the rifle in his hand point downward. It was strange having a gun in his hand on English soil. He had no desire to shoot birds, or to lift a rifle against a living thing ever again. Standing there, waiting for the gamekeeper and the beaters, in company with a row of armed men, reminded him too much of waiting for battle to begin. Though this was different in the fact that this morning was filled with jovial greetings and slaps on the back, which had never happened during the war.

A sense of anticipation filled the air, where before a battle, everyone had been filled with dread, as he'd told Alice. It was strange standing here now. Gentlemanly pursuits hadn't changed while he'd been at war, but something fundamental had changed in Christian, something he didn't think these men would understand. He glanced down the row at the other guests, who weren't paying him any mind. With their excitement and jockeying for bragging rights on who would bag the most birds today, it was unlikely anyone would notice if his rifle remained at his side or that he hadn't brought a servant with him to reload his weapon.

Memories of the war always brought his men's faces to his mind, the ones who had lived, as well as the ones who'd died. Edward's face was at the forefront this morning. Seeing him so affected at the ball, and knowing how easy it was to numb the memories with alcohol, Christian wanted to reach out, to help him. But how? Ever since Christian had come home and fought through the nightmares and temptation of the bottle, he'd thought about his men sharing the same experiences. Nothing was the same coming home, yet they were expected to return to their previous lives as if they hadn't seen soul-crushing panoramas of blood and carnage as they fought for their country. But vocalizing those experiences wasn't acceptable in polite society or at a club.

And yet, he'd spoken to Alice of the circle of brotherhood that formed on the battlefield. What if he could extend the circle of brotherhood he'd once had and bring it home to England? The thought excited him. What if he formed an exclusive gentleman's club for returning veterans, one that encouraged support and sharing? Perhaps a physical refuge could help with the emotional scars and simply having people around who understood could start to heal them. With his new position among the peerage, he had the means to make such an endeavor happen. First, he'd need a property. He'd also need a way to spread the word to those who had served. Christian's mind was racing with ideas.

His thoughts were interrupted with the gamekeeper's shouts, along with the men hired to serve as beaters to force the fowl toward them. Moments later the air was filled with flapping wings as the birds flew into the air in front of him. Gunfire sounded all around him. His stomach clenched, and he looked at Pembroke, but the man was focused on the birds. Christian lifted his face to the sky, watching the fowl that escaped death flying higher as their comrades sank to the earth. The scene was awfully symbolic of Christian's recent thoughts. There were men who were sinking into despair, desperate to escape and find the freedom they'd once fought for. And he was determined to help them.

As the gunfire died down, Christian had the groom fetch his horse. He didn't want to wait for anyone else. Part of him wanted to return to the house right now, find Alice, and tell her all about his idea. She'd barely had a taste of what it meant to do everything you could to survive, only to then suffer repercussions for those actions. She'd understand his desire to extend the battlefield brotherhood to one close to home. But would she want to discuss something so monumental that would distract from capturing the traitor tonight?

She'd said they could have a conversation after the mission was over, and she more than likely meant to converse with him about their connection. But in the time that he'd known her, it was becoming clear that he wanted her opinions and conversation every day, about everything. She had proven intelligent and careful on a variety of subjects he'd never thought to speak of in front of a lady. Her perspective challenged and fascinated him, even when he disagreed. But what did she feel about him?

He was determined to find out. As soon as possible.

CHAPTER 13

*A*lice sat at her dressing table and gave herself one last critical look in the glass. Her blonde hair was twisted into a fashionable chignon with a small sparkling tiara on the crown of her head. Winnie was fussing with a few curled tendrils around her ears, arranging and rearranging them so they would lie just right. Alice's eyes went to her evening gown. The gold color was dazzling and the dress had a rose tinted underlay that gave it an extra shimmer when she walked. It was perfect.

"I think it's fine, Winnie," she said, watching her maid twist a curl once more. "I don't want to be late."

"Yes, my lady." Winnie stepped back, biting her lip.

"You did a wonderful job," Alice told her, patting her on the arm. "You always do."

She stood and the gold silk rustled against her legs, light and smooth as it swirled around her. She reached for her black, jeweled demi-mask and handed it to Winnie so she could tie it on. Nerves fluttered through her middle. This was the night the Falcon Group had been preparing for, and while she was anxious for the masquerade to start, at the same time she wanted it over.

Last night in the kitchen Christian, had talked of waiting for a battle to start with dread and apprehension. Alice would describe her feelings tonight more as an energy she could hardly contain, wanting to get everything settled and over with. Once Pembroke was arrested, they could all breathe a little easier.

"You look beautiful, my lady," Winnie told her. She handed Alice a gold and black matching fan. "There won't be a gentleman who can take his eyes off you."

"You're kind to say so." Alice took the fan and turned toward the door. "Do you think anyone will recognize me?" She pointed to the demi-mask that hid half her face, but left the bottom exposed.

"Not likely, but you stand out wherever you go, my lady." Winnie smiled and turned to begin picking up the extra hairpins from the dressing table.

Alice nodded and let herself out of the room. As she walked to the main staircase, she half hoped Christian would be at the bottom, watching for her. She turned the corner and held her breath.

No one was there.

Swallowing her disappointment, she descended and walked slowly to the ballroom. Guests had already arrived laughing and greeting each other. Some matrons were whispering behind their fans, already looking for some *on dit* to pass along. Alice walked down the hall, caught up in the partial anonymity the costumes provided. Though some guests had worn a simple mask that just covered the eye area and made them easily recognizable, others wore fanciful masks decorated with feathers and crystals that made it impossible to know their identity without other clues. With only a glance, she didn't recognize anyone right away. Her father was right— this was an ideal place for secrets to be shared. Or sold.

With her hand on her middle, Alice moved into the ballroom, where the musicians were tuning their instruments. With some relief, Alice saw her parents right away. Her mother had come with her to the dress fittings, and her sea-blue gown with gold thread was easy to spot. They were near the refreshment table, and she made her way to their side.

After weaving through the small groups of people who had gathered, she finally stopped at her father's elbow. He stood next to her mother, dressed in black, except for a simple white mask. Her mother's demi-mask was outlined with sapphires, emphasizing the blue of her eyes.

"You're a vision," her mother said, reaching over to squeeze her hand. "Like a beautiful sunburst right here in our midst."

"Only eclipsed by you, my sweet," her father put in, raising her mother's hand to his lips. "I am the luckiest man in the kingdom to have such a beautiful wife and daughter."

Alice watched them with a smile on her face. A love match was a rarity among the nobility; she was lucky to have parents who truly cared for each other. Would she be able to find such a treasure for herself? Her feelings for Christian rushed to the surface and her eyes scanned for him again. Would she recognize him? Was he looking for her?

Not seeing him right away, she turned to the refreshment table and picked up a glass of ratafia. Sipping it slowly, she turned and looked over the small groups of guests clustered on the fringes of the ballroom, everyone waiting for the music to begin.

All except one man.

He was standing by a column, half hidden by a large plant, his military bearing unmistakable. And he was watching her. Their eyes met, and she couldn't help the smile that crossed her face.

Christian.

He pushed off the column and started toward her. The anxious nerves that had coiled in her stomach unwound to release butterfly wings through her middle as she watched him approach. He wore a black jacket with a deep-red waistcoat and black breeches. His mask was also red, and, combined with the gleam in his eyes, it was as if the devil himself had approved the costume, marking him as a man with a wicked streak.

One that drew her like a moth to a flame.

She thought of their kiss last night and how her body had responded to his, moving closer and wanting more. Though she'd behaved as a wanton, Alice didn't regret her actions and hoped to repeat them. She flushed at her thoughts, but as if a magnet were pulling her toward him, her feet moved in his direction until they closed the distance between them.

He bent over her hand, lifting it to his lips and letting it linger on her gloved hand. "You are stunning, my lady."

His gaze was warm, and Alice held his words to her heart. "Thank you," she murmured. "You look quite dashing yourself."

Before they could say anything else, her parents moved to the middle of the room to lead out the first dance of the evening. The musicians struck up a waltz, and Christian arched a brow. "Will you do me the honor?"

She nodded and he held out his arm to her. After escorting her to the dance floor, they assumed the waltz position. Her hand slipped into his, and her other rested on his shoulder. Having him so close was heady, and the mass of butterfly wings vibrating through her middle made her breathless. They started moving around the dance floor, and Alice relaxed into his capable arms.

Christian cleared his throat. "I've been thinking about something all day and I wanted to speak with you, but I'm not sure it's the right time," he said, as they twirled around another couple.

Her heart stuttered. Did he want to talk about their connection? The kiss? "This sounds serious," she said, looking up into his eyes.

His hand tightened on hers. "Coming home from the war was difficult for me. I was faced with the death of my elder brother and my father being nearly insensate and bedridden. I had to take over the estate affairs, as well as acclimate to no longer planning battles at night and trying to stay alive by day." He swallowed and took a breath. "I want to help other men who might also be struggling with the adjustment. To extend the brotherhood circle, if you will. I had no one to talk to during my darkest hours, no one who understood. I want to give others the opportunity to have that someone. I think it would help."

"What a splendid idea." She squeezed his hand. "The bonds forged on the battlefield will be extraordinarily helpful. If the men feel safe, they may let their brothers in their circle help them. Were you thinking of a club? Or just holding a regular meeting?"

"A club was foremost in my mind. Somewhere we could relax, have conversation and refreshment, possibly billiards or other diversions, but no gambling or alcohol. A place where the men could find sympathy and solace and still have their pride."

As they made a turn, he drew her closer than was proper, but Alice didn't mind. If they weren't on a ballroom floor, she might be tempted to kiss him. His desire to help his fellow veterans only made her regard for him that much more. "Would you allow all men who served to be members, regardless of rank?"

"There are so many who have served, so I would have to start small, with some sort of requirements for membership. I'm just not sure what they would be quite yet. But you think it's a good idea?" His blue eyes searched hers behind the mask, obviously wanting her thoughts and opinions.

She leaned in, exhilarated at the thought that he cared to know her feelings, his familiar bergamot and mint scent filling her senses. He had dealt with death and anguish, had the marquess title suddenly thrust on him after the devastating loss in his family, and yet he still wanted to reach out to others. He was like no other nobleman she'd ever met.

"Yes, you would have to put some thought into that. I'd love to help you," she said softly. He had a purpose beyond his title, beyond his service in the Falcon Group. Something she herself had been looking for. And he seemed to want her to be part of it.

The song was coming to an end, but she wished it could go on, just to be in his arms a little longer. Out of the corner of her eye, she could see Pembroke watching her on the outskirts of the dance floor. The chances of her speaking privately with Christian for the rest of the evening was small, considering the mission they were trying to accomplish tonight. "I've only been in your circle for a short time, but I know it helped me. I am not surprised at all you would want to help others. And you're the best of men to even attempt it."

As the last chords of the waltz drifted away, he pulled her close to him once more. "Alice, be careful tonight," he said, his voice low and even, sending shivers down her spine. "As soon as this is all over, and the traitor on his way to Newgate, I'd like to have that conversation you promised."

She wanted to press herself to him, run her fingers through his hair, and feel his lips on hers. But instead, she merely smiled and curtsied, hoping he could hear the truth in her tone. "I would like that very much, my lord."

When she rose, Christian escorted her off the dance floor, where Pembroke was waiting. He was dressed in white breeches, a white shirt, waistcoat, and cravat, the lack of color nearly blinding its glory. The only relief from the gleaming white was his robin's egg blue jacket. His white mask was barely covering his eyes and hid nothing about his identity. Pembroke wanted to be recognized.

"May I claim the next dance, my lady?" He bent over her gloved hand and kissed her knuckles.

After being in Christian's arms, part of her wanted to snatch her hand away and pretend she hadn't seen Pembroke. But she was laying a trap for a traitor tonight, and he needed to take the bait. Alice glanced at Christian, who was watching her carefully. This was her role to play. By accepting Pembroke's invitation, she would be able to keep a close eye on him and hopefully thwart the exchange. "I'd be delighted."

The strains of a country dance were just beginning and she took Pembroke's arm. He led her to the dance floor and they took their positions in the line, facing each other. Christian was on the edge of the room, still in her line of sight as he casually leaned against the wall, his arms folded, his eyes on her. He had a casual air, but Alice could feel the restrained power in him. He was ready for anything.

So was she.

She performed the steps of the dance, coming close to Pembroke to make a turn around another couple. "My lady, I have enjoyed furthering our acquaintance at the party this past week," he said when she was at his elbow.

Alice cringed inwardly and thought back to the man she'd once thought he was and used that to hide her true feelings. "You do me a great honor, my lord."

"I'd like to discuss our acquaintance further if you wouldn't mind taking a turn about the gardens." They parted for the dance, but when they came back together, Alice agreed.

"I'm anxious to hear what you have to say," she told him. And she'd be right next to him in case he tried to covertly pass the list to someone.

When the dance ended, he escorted her toward the terrace doors, opening one with a flourish. Before they could cross the threshold, he turned her toward him and took both of her hands in his. "I find I cannot wait, my lady. My feelings for you are those of admiration, but in time they could develop into more and, until then, I feel we would get on well together. I'd like your permission to formally court you and in the near future, be your husband."

He was trembling and speaking so loudly that Alice looked around to make sure no one had overheard them. Since the music and conversation were so loud, no one had paid any attention.

Alice tried to move him through the door and onto the terrace for a modicum of privacy, but he wouldn't budge. How could she answer him? Would he trust her with a traitorous secret if she said yes and accepted his suit? It wouldn't be long before she'd have no choice but to betray him. If she said no tonight, he might leave in a fit of temper and they would lose their chance to catch him and retrieve the list.

"You've caught me by surprise, my lord," she finally said. "I must have a moment to think."

He pulled her hands to his chest, his voice becoming urgent. "Though I've done some things I wish I could take back, I'll shortly be making them right. I would always protect your reputation. You must know that. Your trust and loyalty are everything to me."

But Alice hadn't heard much beyond the admission of things he wished he could take back. What were they? "Can I help you make anything right?" She moved closer to him and looked up into his face, hoping he could still see her sincerity though she was wearing a demi-mask. "You know you can trust me."

He hesitated, as if considering her request, then shook his head. "No, I will take care of this and be worthy of your loyalty. It should all be over tonight." He kissed both her hands and leaned in, his eyes on her lips, as if considering whether to kiss them as well.

Alice pulled back, not wanting him to lose focus, especially if she could get a confession from him. "Whatever do you mean, Lord Pembroke? What exactly will be over tonight? And how can you prove your loyalty to me? Why, a test of loyalty seems straight out of a medieval fairy tale of knights and maidens." She squeezed his hands. "Surely you can speak freely."

Pembroke shook his head and gave her a brittle laugh as if she'd just told a great jest. "If only the complications of the day could be solved with lances and horses. No, my lady, this is not a fairy tale, but I do hope it will have a happy ending. I don't want to say too much, but I'm sure I'll be receiving good news tonight that will

clear any doubt you have about me and my ability to support you."
He looked down at her, his eyes soft and hopeful. "Please tell me
you'll consider it."

"When will you receive this good news?" she asked. Perhaps he
would tell her the time of the meeting. What else could he be
talking about besides getting the money to right his estate and
support her?

"I'm expecting it any minute." He released her. "I'll find you
again the moment I have news, and hopefully you'll have an
answer for me." Stepping back from her, he finally walked through
the door and toward the gardens as if he was in a hurry.

She made to follow him, but another gentleman approached
the doorway, wearing all black except for a white mask. He
blocked Alice's path. "My lady, your father has asked that you stay
close to my side this evening for your protection. I wouldn't want
to disappoint him. Perhaps you'd like to dance?"

"Of course. But Lord Pembroke . . . " Alice glanced back at the
garden where Pembroke had disappeared.

"Never fear, Lord Pembroke will be taken care of," he said
smoothly, overriding her objection.

She nodded, but furrowed her brow as she took his arm. The
man seemed familiar, but she couldn't place him. Her father hadn't
introduced her to many Falcon Group agents in order to keep her
position secret, but maybe she'd seen him with her father before.

She looked over the gentleman's shoulder as they walked to the
middle of the room, hoping to catch Christian's eye, but he was on
the far side of the ballroom, speaking to a footman. Her father had
assured her that Pembroke would be watched carefully all evening,
and he obviously was concerned enough for her safety he'd sent
this agent to her side. She had to trust his experience in these
matters.

The unknown gentleman led her to a corner of the dance floor
as the strains of a quadrille began. Getting into position, she tried

to look closer at her partner's face. His mask covered the top half, revealing only his nose and lips. His eyes were dark and watchful, darting around the room. He was large in stature, though, and Alice was sure she would have remembered him if he'd been a guest at the house party, been in the stables, or posing as a foot-man. Why did he seem so familiar and yet unknown at the same time?

The music began and her partner squeezed her hand, nearly crushing her fingers as they started the first formation. Flexing her wrist, she stared at the buttons on his jacket as she walked with him toward the other couple in their square. Something was pulling at the back of her mind. Where had she seen those buttons before? The style was more like a large bead than a button.

After performing another turn, he pulled her improperly close to his side. Needing some distance, she pushed back, but the man had a death grip on her waist. He stumbled over a step, nearly stomping on her foot.

"My lady, it's not safe. Your father has just given me the signal and I must get you to our prearranged meeting place immediately," he said, his voice soft in her ear. "We must hurry."

Alice tried to twist her head to see her father or Christian. Something was wrong. But the agent didn't allow her any space, quickly making their excuses to the other couples in the square and hurrying her to the door that led to the gardens. Everything inside her was screaming not to let him take her outside. She tried to stop their forward progress by pressing her slippers to the floor and refusing to walk, but her strength was no match for his and he easily lifted her weight with one arm. Fear curled through her veins.

He looked back at her, his dark eyes angry and brooding through his mask. "If you want to live, my lady, come quietly now."

When she felt the press of a gun in her ribs, Alice bit back the protest on her lips. Glancing down, she saw he held a single shot flintlock pistol. Was it coincidence that he had the same gun used in the shooting at the ball in London?

Her stomach sank to her toes as he marched her through the doorway. With the gun in her side, she had no choice but to accompany him out into the night.

CHAPTER 14

Christian had wanted to be at the bottom of the stairs to claim Alice the moment she arrived, but he patiently— though if the tapping of his foot was any indication, rather impatiently— waited for her to appear in the ballroom. When he saw her in the doorway, he resisted the urge to go to her immediately. Her gold dress she wore set her apart, hinting at her daring in being part of the Falcon group, yet the jewels that sparkled in her hair and at her neck accentuated her class and position. She fully owned all parts of herself tonight, and he wanted to share in that.

He couldn't take his eyes off her, and when she smiled at him, he didn't hold himself back any longer. He had to be near her. The moment he'd kissed her hand, the musicians had struck up a waltz, and it was as if the universe was supporting his bid to win this woman's heart. He'd held her closer than he possibly should have, but when she was in his arms, he'd known that they were meant to be partners in every way. Always.

As soon as the dance had ended and Pembroke approached them, Christian had reluctantly relinquished her. The mission was before them, and while there was danger, Christian was determined to stay close and keep Alice as safe as possible. He watched her dancing with Pembroke, their heads bending together whenever the dance steps brought them close. The conversation seemed somewhat serious and Christian wished he could hear what they were saying.

As the dance ended and Pembroke had drawn her toward the terrace doors, Christian had been at the ready should he need to intervene. Alice didn't seem alarmed, though Christian had nearly given in to the urge to plant Pembroke a facer when he was kissing Alice's hands and looked like he might kiss her lips as well. But Christian had stayed back. It was a relief when Pembroke left her alone. Alice was safe for the moment. He watched another man ask for a dance, but before he could ascertain his identity, a footman approached him.

"My lord, you've just received an urgent message," the man said, holding out a folded piece of parchment.

Pulling his eyes away from Alice, Christian impatiently took off his mask, anxious to have his full peripheral vision available. He unfolded the somewhat stained and crumpled paper and saw that he had a drawing in his hands.

The enclosed message was from the artist he'd hired to draw a rendering of the man Ewen the mudlark had seen at Thomas's murder scene. *Ewen says this is as close to a likeness as he can remember. I hope it is helpful in your search, my lord,* the paper read.

Christian had almost given up on getting anything more from the mudlark the day he'd spoken to Nash and heard the skepticism in his voice that Ewen could get past his fear enough to describe the man he'd seen. He'd still sent the artist in the hopes that Nash would convince him. Apparently he had.

Staring down at the drawing, Christian looked for any resemblance to Pembroke, but there wasn't one. The man depicted wasn't Pembroke, but he had some similar features, to be sure. There was something familiar about him, though.

Where had he seen him before?

And then he remembered. The man he'd met in the hallway. Coming out of Pembroke's room before Christian could search it.

The man in the drawing was Pembroke's valet.

All the pieces of the puzzle began clicking into place. A valet was privy to a nobleman's deepest secrets. He had access to correspondence and could overhear conversations from his trusted position. Alice had been right all along. Pembroke was innocent. And they were watching the wrong man tonight.

His eyes darted around the ballroom, past all the dresses that weren't gold. Alice wasn't on the dance floor or the outskirts. Nor was she at the refreshment table. His gut clenched, fear forming like a lead ball in his stomach. She'd accepted a dance with another man when he'd gotten the message. A tall, blonde man, if he recalled correctly. If that was Pembroke's valet, she could be in trouble. He needed to alert the duke.

Striding back to the entryway where the duke and duchess were speaking to some guests, he hurried to their side. The duke looked up and immediately made his way to Christian. "What is it?"

"I've just received a message from one of my informants." He pulled out the drawing and showed it to the duke. "This is a rendering of the man who I believe murdered Thomas Norwich and is our traitor. It's Pembroke's valet. He was last seen in Alice's company, but they have both disappeared." His heart pounded against his ribs. Where was she? Was she hurt?

The duke put his hand on Christian's shoulder. "I have guards at all the entrances and agents in every part of the house and stables. We'll find her." He went back to his wife and whispered in her ear. She paled, but nodded.

Coming back to Christian's side, the duke led the way to the terrace with Christian on his heels. Once they were outside, Christian made note of the couples quietly talking. None of them were Alice. The torch lights led down to gardens, where he could see some shadows moving through the darkness. But Langdon Park was an extensive estate. They needed a plan to search effectively.

"Where would he have taken her?" Christian asked, panic surging in him. He had to tamp down his emotions and think critically. Her life might depend on it. This man had already made two attempts to kill her. Christian clenched his fists. He had to find her before the unthinkable happened.

The duke touched his shoulder as if reading his thoughts. "Alice is armed and has a cool head in difficult situations. We just need to find her."

Christian remembered her crouching in Pembroke's room, her dagger at the ready and the bands of worry squeezing his lungs unwound a bit. "I think we need to separate to cover more ground. What if you check the gardens? I'll check the stables."

The duke was scanning the area around them. "I had several agents on the terrace as well as the perimeter of the garden, but I don't see any of them now." A thread of worry crept into his voice. "Perhaps they're on her trail and we just need to catch up." He headed down the stone steps into the garden. "I'll send word the moment I find them."

Christian hoped the duke was right, and that Alice would be found momentarily. He took the gravel path that led to the stables, his long strides eating up the ground. When he burst into the stable, the groom near the door jumped back.

"Can I help you, my lord?" the man asked, quickly tugging on his forelock.

"I'm looking for the Earl of Pembroke," Christian announced, pacing up and down, looking into the stalls and corners, anywhere the valet could have hidden Alice. "Is his carriage still here?"

"No, my lord. The earl left a while back with Lady Alice and his valet." The groom's cheeks reddened. "He weren't feeling well."

Christian stepped closer to the man, concern for Alice's safety taking hold of him again. "What do you mean he wasn't well?"

"His valet was nearly holding the earl up. Said he'd had too much to drink and embarrassed himself. The lady was kind enough to offer to help sober him up so they could return to the party." The groom moved back. "I hope I haven't spoken out of turn."

Pembroke must have been drugged. That was the only explanation. At least Alice seemed to be well for the moment. "No, you haven't spoken out of turn. Did the valet say where he was taking the earl?" Christian needed to find them before the situation turned any more dangerous than it already was.

The groom shifted his weight from foot to foot. "No, my lord. But the coachman was unhappy to be ordered about by a valet. He'd been told to keep the carriage hitched for the earl so he could take a meeting tonight and be back before the ball was over. The coachman grumbled loud and long to all of us about having to drive an hour away to the Rose and Crown."

That had to be where the meeting to sell the agent list was going to take place. "You need to inform the duke," he said to the groom.

"Yes, my lord." But before the groom could move past him, they heard shouts coming from the side of the stables. The tension Christian was feeling ratcheted up. Had the duke found something?

They walked around the corner in time to see the duke carrying another man over his shoulders. "We need to get him inside." Several stable hands came out to help lower the unconscious man to the ground. "He's been shot and his partner as well." The duke leaned over, his hands on his knees. "Someone call for my physician. Immediately."

Christian clenched his fists. He turned on his heel and went back into the stable. He needed to saddle Prince immediately.

Pembroke's valet had a gun and had already shot two men. He'd probably threatened Alice as well to get her to leave with him. Rage fired his blood. The man obviously had planned this operation down to the smallest detail and expected to get away with it.

But Christian would die before he let that happen.

He had to get to Alice.

CHAPTER 15

*A*lice sat back in her carriage seat. She'd been shocked when Pembroke's valet had removed his mask and she'd recognized him. So many things made sense now— and her instinct that Pembroke was innocent had been right. If only she could have gotten a message to Christian. But with a gun at her back, Alice had to go along with whatever the valet had planned.

Her gaze landed on Pembroke. He was in the corner of the coach, his hands tied and a gag in his mouth. He was moaning and barely conscious.

"What have you done to him?" Alice asked, proud that her voice didn't waver. She carefully removed her mask and put it next to her leg.

"With the blow to the head and the tincture he was given, he should have been felled like an oak. Obviously my brother should have hit him harder or given him more," the valet grumbled, wrinkling his nose. Pembroke groaned and his eyes rolled back in his head. His valet just gave him another disdainful look. "Pompous fool."

Grateful she hadn't been gagged and tied, she rubbed her arms as gooseflesh appeared over her skin. The night was chilly, and the silk did nothing to protect her against the cold or the fear pricking her heart. Since they'd left the ball, Pembroke's valet had shot both agents trying to stop them from getting to the stables, then turned the gun toward her. She'd held her hands up in surrender. The valet had collected Pembroke's nearly unconscious form by the back gate, and then they'd hurried to the stables where the carriage was waiting. She still couldn't get the smell of blood and gunpowder out of her nose. "Why are you doing this? Are you hoping for ransom?"

"It's not just about the money. You nobs are always playing with people's lives, and don't think about anyone but yourselves. Servants are nothing more than chattel to be used, then thrown away like rubbish." He scowled at Pembroke, gripping the gun tighter. Alarm was growing in Alice's heart. Judging from the bloodlust in his eyes, he planned to kill them both.

"If you're unhappy in your position with Lord Pembroke, I could speak to my father. Perhaps find a place for you at Langdon Park," she offered.

He let out a bitter laugh. "It's not about position, you fool! My family, most especially my mother, have suffered every indignity because of people like you." He turned in the seat, his gun pointing toward her. Alice tried to quell the fear, looking at his face instead of the gun.

"What happened to your family?" She kept her voice soft, hoping to calm his rage, maybe make him see reason.

He stared at her for a moment, pressing a hand to his temple. "My little brother went off to war, proud to serve his country. Wellington himself saw how fleet of foot he was and used him to track enemy troop movements. But my brother wasn't quick enough and ended up with his throat slit behind enemy lines." The valet's voice shook and he lifted the gun to Pembroke's heart. "All my mother got was a letter of regret from the army and

'Your country thanks you for your sacrifice'—but they killed him!"

"Your brother died honorably, helping to win the war. Many mothers received the same letter." The knife was in the hidden sheath at her waist, but it wouldn't protect her against a gun. But if she could keep him talking until he met with his buyer, there might be a chance to somehow foil the sale of the list. She needed to try.

"My brother was expendable. The son of a gardener. Who would miss a servant? They thought no one would care, but I'm going to *make* them care," he snarled.

The coach came to a stop, and the valet looked over at her. "I'm going to escort you into the inn, just the same as we went to the stables. We are helping the Earl of Pembroke in his time of need." He opened the door. "And if you try to run or ask for help, remember that I have no good will toward British Intelligence Officers or the upper classes at the moment. I will shoot you, then perhaps leave you behind in a field like they did my brother."

Alice shivered at the image, but inclined her head. "I understand." She didn't plan to antagonize him. This was the chance Falcon Group had been waiting for since the moment Thomas had been killed, and she had a chance to finish the mission.

The valet shouldered Pembroke's weight, as if he were helping his drunk master find his bed, as they made their way across the inn's courtyard. As they walked toward the entrance of the inn, a man dismounted from his horse and came to them immediately. With his similar features, it was easy to see he was the brother the valet had spoken of who had struck Pembroke and given him a tincture. And since he was wearing an apron and walked like he owned the property, it seemed he was the innkeeper here.

The brother stopped in front of them. "Jasper." He looked at her, then turned his face and lowered his voice. "I made sure that one of the girls readied your usual bedchamber upstairs for you with a private parlor. Lock them in the chamber for safekeeping, and then you can wait for our . . . um . . . guest, in the parlor. I'll bring you something to drink."

Ah, the valet's name was Jasper. Alice filed that information away. Jasper grunted his assent and readjusted Pembroke's weight before he headed for the stairs, motioning for her to walk in front of him. She could feel several patrons' eyes on her, but she ducked her head, not wanting to meet their eyes. Alice needed to stay close to Jasper.

"First room on the right," Jasper said, hauling Pembroke up the stairs none too gently.

Alice opened the door and stepped inside. It was a small room with a bed in the corner and a chair in front of the fireplace. Jasper came in after her and unceremoniously dropped Pembroke on the bed.

"The fool had no idea he was being framed. Just sulked and pouted about being given the cut direct by his supposed *friends*." He snorted in disgust. "All he cared about was himself."

Alice looked at Pembroke, remembering his distress at the rumors besmirching his family name. "He was worried about losing his home and how the rumors were affecting his mother and sister," she said softly. "Surely you can understand that."

"No one cared about my mum or sister and how losing Freddie affected them." Jasper snapped. "We didn't even have a body for a proper Christian burial. Now sit in the chair."

Alice sat, watching warily as Jasper approached her while taking off his cravat. The gold buttons on the coat winked at her again. That's where she'd seen them before. In Pembroke's dressing room when they'd searched the pockets of his jacket. He obviously felt comfortable in his master's clothing, and they were of a similar height and build.

"What do you plan to do with me?" she asked, trying to prolong the conversation, hoping he would feel comfortable enough to reveal his plans.

"I'm going to attend a very important meeting that will make me a rich man." He went around the chair and yanked both arms painfully behind her. Using the cravat, he tied her wrists tightly. "When I'm through making Wellington's spies pay, I'll offer you and the earl to the French. Everyone in Britain will think you've run off together. I'm sure the French could find a use for a duke's daughter who has shamed herself by spying, and a useless English noble." He laughed cruelly. "You know, maybe the French had the right of it in getting rid of all the nobility."

Alice bowed her head and sniffed as if she were fighting back tears. Jasper pulled on the knot before he straightened. "Now use the manners that every gently bred *lady* is taught and sit here quietly until I come for you."

Alice didn't look at him. She kept her eyes dutifully on the floor until the door was closed and she heard it lock behind him. Then she started working on her bindings. One thing she'd practiced relentlessly had been escaping any sort of bonds. Her father had made it a game to tie her hands in exotic knots as well as serviceable ones, and, while some had taken longer to get free from than others, she'd always managed it. One more talent she could never divulge to her friends.

Pulling her shoulders back, she tried to feel the shape of the knot Jasper had tied. This one was complicated, but she was confident it wouldn't take long before she was free. She had to get to that parlor.

Pulling and pushing the sides of the knot, testing what tightened and what loosened with each action was painstaking work. Feeling the knots coming loose under her fingers brought a satisfied smile to her face, but getting out of the bindings had still taken a little longer than she had anticipated. She breathed a relieved sigh when she was finally free.

Stretching her fingers and rolling her wrists, she stood and looked over at Pembroke. He had stopped moaning and was now snoring on the bed. There would be no help from him. She was on her own.

Pressing her ear to the door, Alice didn't hear anything from outside. With a pat of the back of her hair, she took two hairpins out, then fashioned one into an L-shape and used the other as a straight pick. The lock gave way easily and Alice slowly opened the door. The corridor was empty.

Her slippers were quiet on the wood floor, but she still tiptoed to the front of the parlor doors. The voices inside were soft, but one was unmistakably French. The exchange had begun.

Alice took a deep breath. Surely her father and Christian had noticed her absence by now. They would be looking for her, and hopefully the groom or one of the agents could give them clues as to where she'd been taken. Holding onto that hope, she moved forward.

Just stall the proceedings until they get here, she told herself.

Taking a breath, she decided to play the role of a jealous mistress. Hopefully she could keep up the ruse long enough for her father and Christian to arrive. With one last exhale, she quietly opened the door to the parlor.

Both men turned at her entrance. Jasper's eyes narrowed, and he started toward her. She moved out of his reach toward the Frenchman. "Don't come near me," she warned Jasper. "You're nothing but an oath-breaker."

"What is the meaning of this?" the Frenchman said, motioning toward her. He looked like a dandy, with lace cuffs and a cravat that boasted an emerald stickpin.

Alice turned to address him. "I came to tell you, *monsieur*, that you have been betrayed. Jasper has told the English that you are here, and they are coming to arrest you. After your exchange, he means to ply you with food and wine until they arrive." Alice looked directly at Jasper. "He is a greedy man with his women and his ways. The English pay well." She gave a delicate shrug.

Jasper's jaw went slack and he sputtered in shock. "She's lying! She's one of them spies. Her name is on the list. You can read it on the first page."

"Why would you tell me of his plan, *mon petite?*" The Frenchman moved closer to her, but she stayed just out of his reach. "Though if what he says is true, the English have improved the ranks of their spies." He gave her an appreciative glance.

Brushing her hands down her hips, she hoped to distract him enough that he wouldn't think too closely about her words. "I'm an abigail for the daughter of the house, and Jasper caught my eye." She lowered her gaze to the floor. "I allowed him a few liberties, and for the last few months he's written me poetry and given me gifts of fine clothing. He promised to marry me and spirit me away, but instead, he played me for the fool." She glared at Jasper and didn't have to put on act of anger toward him. It was all too real. "Now I find out he has given two maids the same promises."

Jasper's face was red, as if he were about to have an apoplexy. "She's lying. Look at her. She's not a servant!"

She drew herself up to her full height and shook her finger in Jasper's direction. "I am what you made me— a scorned woman!"

The Frenchman looked between them, putting a finger underneath his chin. "I cannot decide which one of you is lying, so I will take my leave since our business is concluded."

Alice nearly gasped at his words. He already had the list! She couldn't let him go now.

She watched him move toward the door, and pulled her dagger out, but before she could do anything, Jasper was shaking his head and blocking the Frenchman's way. "I need to make sure all the money is accounted for, Dubois. You're not leaving until I do."

Dubois rolled his eyes. "Ah. You English have such terrible manners. You can count it after I leave."

"No." Jasper pointed his gun toward Dubois's abdomen. "You'll wait. I'll not be cheated by you."

In the blink of an eye, Dubois had pinned Jasper to the wall and pounded his head into it until the man slumped to the ground unconscious. Dubois wasn't large, but he was obviously powerful. Alice wouldn't underestimate him.

He straightened his lace cuff. "I must say *au revoir*, my lady," he told her with a shrewd glance. "Unless you have something else to offer me?"

"I'm afraid I need the list in your possession," she said firmly, holding her dagger in her hand. Not taking her eyes off him, she pressed her lips together, sizing him up. He was a little taller than her, lean, but sure of himself. That could work to her advantage. "I can't let you leave with it."

He glanced at the dagger and let out a long, dramatic sigh. "*Cherie*, I was hoping you wouldn't say that. I was moved by your story of broken promises, but they were lies. Now I see that you are, in fact, are a very beautiful spy. Sadly, one that will die tonight." Pulling his own dagger from his boot, he slowly moved toward her, shaking his head. "I will have you know I won't enjoy this."

"But I will." Her grip on her knife was loose, but ready.

This was it.

His dagger was slightly larger than hers, but that wasn't what mattered. Knife-fighting was about speed and disabling one's opponent as quickly as possible. Alice's heart pounded so hard in her veins that blood was rushing through her ears, making it hard to hear.

Focus. Breathe.

She stayed on the balls of her feet as they circled each other warily. The blade was above her thumb, shining in the firelight. Alice calmed her mind, keeping to her fencing stance, concentrating entirely on Dubois. Her father's words echoed through her head. "Aim to slice a large muscle to immobilize. Keep your defenses up."

Dubois feinted toward one side, but Alice matched his steps. Her skirts were a nuisance, but she didn't have an extra hand to use to sweep them up. He lunged forward and Alice quickly side-stepped him, but had the presence of mind to slice her knife through the air. She made contact.

He drew his forearm back with a hiss, his eyes wide that she'd drawn blood first. "You've been trained well."

Alice didn't acknowledge his words. They were still doing a strange dance, moving in a half-circle, staying the same distance apart. Alice had the added difficulty of not tripping over Jasper's inert form or her gown.

Seeing her dilemma, Dubois's gaze was distracted and drawn to her feet for a moment. Seizing the opportunity, Alice lunged forward, slashing his thigh. The razor- sharp dagger pierced through fabric and skin, leaving a large gash in his breeches. Blood rushed from the wound.

"*Sacre bleu!*" he muttered, stumbling toward her.

She tried to move back, but Jasper's body didn't give her any space. With her attention diverted, Dubois was on her in a trice, slashing at her right shoulder.

Alice gasped. Pain seared through her and she nearly dropped her dagger, but instead, she gripped it tightly, swept her arm in a small arc for momentum, and plunged her knife into his side.

He groaned and fell to the ground near Jasper. Struggling to rise, he was moving toward the door when Alice grabbed his hair and held her blade to his throat. "It's over," she said, breathing heavily. "Give me your weapon, or I'll finish what I've started."

His dagger clattered to the floor. "I never thought an English woman would be talented with a blade."

She kicked his dagger away, keeping her weapon pressed to his pulse. "The French usually underestimate the English. Now, kneel."

She stayed behind him, with her blade pressed to the artery in his neck— an uncomfortable reminder that with a flick of her wrist, his blood would be all over the floor.

"I'll take that list now. And then you have an appointment. With the British Foreign Office." She couldn't reach into his jacket pocket and get it herself. Her own blood was trickling down her arm, and she didn't know if she had enough strength to reach for it. She hoped he wouldn't call her bluff.

"You'll have to take it from me," the Frenchman said. "With the honor I have left, I will not freely give it to you."

She bent close to his ear, the smell of wine and blood permeating his clothing. "You will have everything taken from you. Your name, your operation, everything that identifies you will be made known to the British. But your honor will not be taken." She shook her head. "We can't take what you never had."

The dagger tip pressed deeper into his skin and a drop of blood fell and trickled down his neck. She held his life in her hands. But she would not end it.

Because she knew what true honor was.

CHAPTER 16

*C*hristian rode neck-for-nothing to get to the Rose and Crown. Just before he reached the general vicinity, he slowed down. He couldn't ride in there lathered and spent. He had to be smart and think through the consequences of his actions. He didn't want to do anything to endanger Alice further.

As he approached the courtyard, a boy around the age of ten came out of the stables, rubbing his eyes as if he'd just woken up. "Can I 'elp you, milord?"

"If you get my horse some water and walk him around the courtyard until I get back, there's a crown in it for you," Christian said as he dismounted.

The boy's eyes widened. "Yes, milord." He took the reins and patted Prince's nose. "Come with me," he told the horse as he walked away.

Christian took stock of the courtyard and was relieved when he saw the Pembroke carriage in the far corner. That likely meant Alice was still here. Christian took a deep breath to calm his pulse. Looking closer, he could see the coachman leaning against the carriage, taking a drink from a flask. Christian walked over. He wanted some answers.

The coachman eyed him as he got closer, wiping his lips on his sleeve. "Have you come for the lady?" he asked without preamble.

Christian covered his surprise at the coachman's bluntness. "Yes." He stood in front of the man and folded his arms. "What can you tell me about what's happened?"

The coachman turned his head and spit in the dirt beside them. "That valet, Jasper is his name, has been ordering everyone around, acting like he's Quality and not a servant like the rest of us. Came to me with some faradiddle about Lady Alice trying to spare the earl embarrassment by bringing him here to sober up." He barked out a laugh. "Like a duke's daughter would be going to an inn during her own party. And without her maid!" The coachman looked at Christian. "I thought it all a bit havey-cavey and made sure that groom in the duke's stables heard where we were going. I was hoping someone would come for the lady."

Christian inclined his head. "You have my thanks. How long have they been inside?"

"Not long, but you'd best hurry." The coachman took another swig from his flask. "Lady Alice is known for her kindness to everyone, no matter what their class. I'd hate to see her hurt in any way."

Christian took his leave, turning on his heel to walk toward the entrance of the inn. With a glance in the downstairs windows, he didn't see anyone resembling Alice. His gut clenched and the feeling he needed to hurry intensified. He ran a hand through his windblown hair, trying to figure out the best way to find her. If he burst inside, that might call undue attention to himself and put Alice in more danger by forcing Jasper into a standoff.

No, he'd go around to the back.

Creeping around the side of the inn, the moon gave off barely enough light to make out the shadow of the back entrance.

Opening the door, he slipped inside and found himself in a small hallway between the kitchen and the common room. A staircase was across the way. Just as he moved toward the stairs, a large man pushed through the kitchen door and nearly barreled into him.

The man stumbled back and let out a frustrated grunt, "What the—" he started, before he looked at Christian. Quickly schooling his face into a pleasant expression, he wiped his hands on his apron. "My lord, what can I do for you? I'm afraid the rooms are full for this evening, but I can offer you a warm lamb stew."

He turned toward the light and smiled. Christian froze at the sight. Tall. Blonde. A longish nose. This man could nearly be the valet's twin.

That's why Jasper had chosen this inn as the exchange place. He had relatives here. Ones that would help him.

Christian grabbed the man's shirtfront and slammed him against the wall. "You so closely resemble the Earl of Pembroke's valet, that I can only assume you are an accomplice to his plans. Treason is a hanging offense, if you didn't know. And I will make sure you hang right next to him." He let the man go, but stayed close. "Where did he take her?"

The inn owner held his neck, gaping at Christian. "Jasper took them upstairs. First door on the right," he said, his voice trembling. "But I haven't done anything worth hanging over. I only provided a room and a parlor. No harm in that."

"You can state your case to the magistrate." Christian turned and took the stairs two at a time. He carefully opened the first door on the right. As he walked in, he noted the empty chair by the fireplace and an unconscious Pembroke on the bed. Walking closer, he stood over Pembroke's pale form. Had they left him for dead?

He had to find Alice.

Walking back into the hall, Christian went next door to the adjoining parlor. The door was closed. Christian tried to push it open, but something heavy was blocking the other side. Throwing his shoulder into it, he finally pried the door open enough that he could get in. Stepping over the valet's unconscious form lying in front of the door, he turned his attention to the other two people in the room.

And for the first time since Alice had disappeared, he smiled.

She had the Frenchman on his knees, her dagger to his throat. "About time you arrived," she said, breathing heavily. "He has the list in his pocket."

Christian hurried forward, reaching into the man's jacket pocket and taking the list out. After a cursory glance at it, he tucked it into his own pocket. Once it was safely in his possession, he drew the Frenchman to his feet.

"Did he hurt you?" he asked, looking Alice over from head to toe.

"I'm fine," she said, but blood on her arm belied her words. Her gaze followed his as she looked down at the wound. "It's a scratch."

Christian looked at her arm and torn dress. Anger fired through his veins. He twisted the Frenchman's wrist behind his back until he cried out in pain. "If I didn't know what was already in store for you, I'd kill you myself," he said in the man's ear.

"I'm afraid the lady already has," the Frenchman moaned as the blood from his leg wound dripped on the floor. "You will be spared the privilege of hanging me."

"You won't die that easily, *monsieur.*" The Duke of Huntingdon and two other agents walked through the door, inching the valet's body farther into the room. The duke looked down at Jasper, then up at Alice and Christian as he took in the scene. "Dubois. Let me properly welcome you to British soil. I never thought to see you so far from your master's side. It will be an honor to bring the first lieutenant of the French secret police to my superiors."

Dubois roared his frustration and tried to lunge for the duke's neck, but fell weakly at his feet instead. The duke stood over him for a moment, then, with a flick of his wrist, motioned the two agents forward. "Take him to the coach and make sure he is securely chained. I will be there shortly."

The agents nodded, then each one moved to either side of Dubois. Taking him by the arms, they dragged him from the room. Once they were gone, the duke went to Alice's side.

"I was worried," he said, his voice gruff as he held out her wounded arm. "But apparently it was for naught. You've done well."

She moved closer to her father and smiled. "Papa, I was right about Pembroke. He was innocent. His valet, Jasper framed him because his little brother was killed spying for Wellington." Alice's forehead creased as she looked down at her arm. "Winnie is going to be cross with me. There's blood on my gown and she says it's nearly impossible to get out of silk."

Her father kissed her forehead, letting out a relieved breath. "I'm going to have to make arrangements for Jasper and his brother. They have a bit of explaining to do." He turned to Christian. "Would you see my daughter home?"

"Of course, Your Grace." He offered his elbow to Alice, and she took it with her good arm. He put his other hand over hers, grateful to have her at his side again.

They walked down the narrow stairs, her steps slow and measured. "Is your ankle paining you?" he asked, "or your shoulder?"

"No, I just don't want to trip on my gown and fall down the stairs at your feet." She darted a glance at Christian and he laughed.

"You're worried about swooning at my feet?" He leaned in and raised his brows, enjoying the blush spreading across her cheeks. "Because you think I'm so handsome?"

She pushed away from him slightly, letting out a disgruntled puff of air. "What a vexing rogue you are."

"So you don't deny it?" He pulled her close to him as she shook her head in mock dismay. He laughed again and kissed the top of her head. "Don't worry, I won't let you fall," he assured her. "Whether you think I'm handsome or not."

Alice rolled her eyes, but they did manage to reach the landing at the bottom of the stairs safely. Once they were near the back hallway, Christian steered her into the kitchen. No one was inside and the inn was eerily quiet. Presumably, the duke had taken the innkeeper into his custody, and the downstairs portion of the inn had closed when they left. Either way, he wanted to take care of Alice whether or not anyone was about.

Sitting her down on a stool, he turned to the cupboard and took down a bottle of whisky. After pulling out his handkerchief, he tore it in two.

"What are you doing?" she asked with an amused smile, color high in her cheeks.

"Taking care of you." He gently lifted her arm. The fabric of her dress had been cut cleanly from the shoulder to the elbow. Pulling apart the threads that were barely holding the sleeve together, he bared her arm. The cut didn't look deep, but would need to be cleaned and dressed.

"My father's physician can do it." She looked down at her arm and bit her lip, quickly turning her face away. "I didn't realize there was quite so much blood."

He touched her under the chin and gently turned her face until she looked into his eyes. "The sooner we disinfect the cut, the harder it will be for infection to set in. I'd rather do this now."

She nodded and Christian let his thumb trace her jaw, wishing he could take the pain away for her. "This is going to hurt a bit. I'm sorry." Quickly, before she could think about it, he poured the whisky on the cut, catching the excess with one half of his handkerchief.

She ground her teeth together and whimpered, but no other

sound escaped. Christian worked quickly. In the field, staving off fevers and infection had been the biggest priority. Many men had received minor wounds, only to die from the infection that set in afterward. He wasn't about to let that happen to Alice.

Once the wound was clean, he bound it with the other half of his handkerchief. Tying it off with a small bow, he bent over and kissed it. She touched his hair, her hands running over his head, soothing him, then guiding him upward until his mouth touched hers. Tasting her lips, and being close enough to feel her against him warm and whole, made this kiss something he'd never felt before. All the pulse-pounding anxiety and fear easily turned to passion and yearning for the woman in front of him. He couldn't get enough.

Letting his hands rove over her back, he pulled her to a standing position and pressed her closer. "Alice," he said, savoring her name as he imprinted little kisses from her jaw to her ear. "I thought I'd lost you."

"Never." She arched against him and tried to slide her arms around his neck, but pulled back with a hiss. "Oh, my arm," she said, wincing. "I'm sorry."

"Forgive me for forgetting myself." He gave her one last chaste kiss before he stepped back. "We need to get you home."

"I didn't mind," she said with a saucy grin.

Christian looked down at her and the moment froze in time. There she was, in a stranger's kitchen, her dress torn and bloodied after a battle, but with a smile on her face. Her courage and zest for life made him want to hold her against him and never let her go. This was a night that would be impressed upon his mind forever.

She was brilliant.

He kept her arm in his and walked her carefully to the back door. With one last glance around, Christian led her through the shadow-darkened path to the courtyard. When they turned the corner, they nearly came face-to-nose with Prince. The boy walking him around the perimeter grinned when he saw Christian.

"I held him, just like you asked, m'lord," the lad said.

Christian pulled a crown out of his pocket and gave it to the boy. "You earned it, lad."

The boy took the money and stared at it a moment before he put it in his pocket. "Wait until I show my ma!" And he ran off.

Christian took off his greatcoat and put it around Alice, turning her so he could fasten it at her neck. It fell nearly to her ankles. "I rode here as fast as I could. I've never been so frightened in my life. I can't help but think if only I'd arrived sooner, you might not have been hurt."

She looked up at him, her eyes bright. "I knew you'd come for me. I stayed calm as best I could and tried to remember my training. I think I surprised Dubois."

Christian chuckled and shook his head. "I don't doubt you did. You've surprised me from the moment I met you. And tonight you single-handedly saved the list and thwarted a traitor. You should get a medal."

"For now, I'd like a warm bath." She leaned into him, and Christian held her close with one arm, the other rubbing her back in soothing circles.

"Will you ride with me? Or should I ask for Pembroke's carriage to be readied?" Christian knew what he wanted her to choose, but waited for her answer.

She grinned. "We've come this far. I want to see it through to the end. And I must say, it seems fitting that we ride back to Langdon Park together. Too bad we can't sport a victory flag of some sort."

The corners of his mouth turned up as he pulled her close. "We make a good team," he said. "And I don't think I want that to end."

Alice reached out and pushed his hair back from his forehead. "Neither do I."

He bent down and claimed her lips. She had battled tonight and won. She was wounded, but alive, and his pulse thrummed through him as he pressed her closer. Alice returned his kiss with fervor, her lips branding him, as she slowly and carefully threaded her good hand through his hair. All the worry and fear that had run through his veins tonight melted away. It was only her. Her sweet scent of rosewater was now mixed with the faint smell of blood— another testament of her strength and character.

She'd proven herself a hero tonight. And whether he was the one handing her a weapon or standing at her side to fight, he knew he always wanted her with him.

Together. Always. In victory or defeat.

CHAPTER 17

*A*lice burrowed her nose into Christian's greatcoat, the bergamot and mint scent giving her a sense of comfort. Prince carried both of them without any effort, and it wouldn't be long before she was home. For now, though, she was enjoying being warm and safe with Christian's solid presence at her back and his arms surrounding her.

She leaned into him and turned her head. "You know, when I finally realized what was happening, and that the valet was the traitor, my first thought was, I was right about Pembroke being innocent."

"Yes, your instincts were right on." He tightened his arms around her. "The day we went shooting I spoke with him and started to doubt his guilt as well. The evidence was just so over-whelming, I couldn't see how he could explain that away."

"Jasper did a thorough job in framing him." Alice shifted her weight. "I hope the drugs Pembroke was given don't do any permanent damage."

"I'm sure your father will have a lot of questions for him when he's lucid." Christian's breath tickled her neck and sent tingles down her spine. She couldn't stop thinking about the kisses they'd shared in the kitchen and the courtyard. He'd come for her. Believed in her. And she wanted him to be hers.

"Does *your* father know what you do for the Falcon Group?" Alice kept her voice low and soft. Was his family difficult to talk about?

"I think he guessed after a while." Christian's voice trailed off. "The three of us—my brother, my father, and me—were so close after my mother died. My father would talk over the parliamentary matters he was involved with, and my brother talked about the estate. Endlessly." He chuckled. "When we were at home together, we hunted and fished, and when we were apart, we wrote each other regularly." His voice got very soft, barely more than a murmur. "They both knew their place in the world, but it took me longer to find mine. And now that I have, I must give it up. Family always comes first." Christian straightened in his seat and shifted her closer to him. "Not that I mind, really. I just feel most useful and able to contribute my skills in military and intelligence matters."

"You haven't lost your place and purpose. It's just changing a bit." She twisted so she could meet his eyes. "You're going to help the men coming home from the war, and you're in a unique position to help change the laws of our country to do more for them as well. And you still have Falcon Group, though your role might be different now."

He kissed the end of her nose. "I love how you think. You see things so clearly, and you help me see things differently as well," he said in her ear. "You're unlike every other woman I've ever met."

"I'll assume you mean that as a compliment." She smiled and turned forward once again.

"Most definitely a compliment." He leaned forward, his lips nuzzling the nape of her neck. "When we realized you'd been taken, I was so worried, but your father reassured me that you were armed and capable. And you were."

His kisses were featherlight, but they started a firestorm in her middle. "I was still glad to see you walk into that parlor," she said, a mite breathlessly.

"With my brother's death and my father's illness . . . I couldn't lose you as well." He kissed her earlobe and she closed her eyes, wishing they weren't on horseback. "You've become so important to me in such a short time."

She gazed up at him and tilted her face just enough to kiss the edge of his mouth. "You're important to me, too."

The lights of Langdon Park were just ahead, and Alice sighed. She wanted more time. Right here, on the back of the horse, with only stars as their witness, everything seemed how it should be. This was where she wanted to stay. If only she could.

There were no carriages in front of the mansion, and the house was quiet, so the masquerade guests must have all gone home. Two grooms came out to meet them as they approached. Christian dismounted, then gently lifted her down. She swayed toward him, and he quickly handed off the reins off to a groom and swept her into his arms. Her excitement had given way to exhaustion, so Alice laid her head against his chest and closed her eyes.

The butler opened the door as they gained the top step and Alice's mother was in the entryway. "Oh, Alice!" she exclaimed, rushing to her side. "Take her to the drawing room."

"I'm all right, Mama," Alice said, but her voice sounded small in the large entryway. The duchess probably hadn't heard.

Once in the parlor, Christian set her down on the green damask sofa, then promptly took the seat beside her. She laid her head against his shoulder as her mother sat in the chair right next to her and dismissed all the servants.

"What happened?" the duchess asked when they were alone,

discreetly wiping away a tear. "I was so worried when your father said he was going to find you."

Alice looked over at her mother. "Lord Pembroke's valet was framing him for Thomas's murder and for being a traitor to the Crown." Her arm was starting to throb. "He was beside himself after his brother died in the war, spying behind enemy lines for Wellington. He wanted revenge, so he was going to make everyone think I had run off with Lord Pembroke, then sell us to the French."

Christian's body tensed as she spoke. She lightly touched the back of his hand. "It all ended well, though." Her eyes were starting to close. She was feeling so very tired all of a sudden.

"Your daughter was magnificent. She kept her head about her and managed to foil all his plans." Christian's voice rumbled through her and Alice sighed.

The door opened and her father strode in. He walked to his wife's side immediately and kissed her cheek. "I'm sorry to have worried you, my dear," he said softly. "It couldn't be helped."

She sniffed. "I agreed to all your extra activities from your very first assignment all those years ago, and I know your work is important," she said, softening the admonishment with a small smile. "But I do worry."

Alice opened her eyes and found her father's gaze. "Where is Dubois? And Jasper?"

"We took them to the Priest House on the far side of the estate. It hasn't been used in years and is in a bit of disrepair, but there are several rooms without windows, and doors that lock from the outside. It's the most secure building we have until we can get them back to London." Her father sat down in a chair opposite her mother. "How are you feeling, Alice?"

"Tired." She looked over at Christian. "Relieved." Turning back to her father, she straightened. "Has Dubois or Jasper said anything?"

"My physician is with Dubois now. It wouldn't do for him to bleed to death before I can deliver him to the Foreign Office. He hasn't said a word. Jasper is very anxious to talk, however. He claims he never meant to harm you at all, that he only wanted money for his mother, to ease her pain and suffering after the loss of her son. Though if you ask him about Thomas or the Earl of Pembroke, he's not very complimentary. Nothing I can repeat in the presence of ladies, you understand." He winked at Alice. "Not that you would want to hear it anyway."

"What happens now?" the duchess asked, twisting her handkerchief in her hands. "Will they be here much longer?"

"No, my dear. I will have them moved as soon as I can make arrangements." He stood and touched his wife's shoulder. "I won't have them here a moment longer than necessary."

Her mother stood with him, patting his hand. "Thank you, Edmund. Now, we need to get Alice in bed. I'll ring for Winnie and make sure to have Cook make a posset for you. It will all look better in the morning."

"Yes, Mama." Alice felt Christian's arms come around her again.

"Perhaps I should assist her upstairs. The shock seems to have set in." Christian pressed her close, and Alice sighed into his warmth. He always seemed warm. Or was making her feel warm.

"Thank you." The duke held the door open for them, and the duchess led the way.

"I'd like to meet with you tomorrow morning, Your Grace," Christian said as he passed by with Alice.

"Yes, I think you should," the duke said, nodding as they gained the hallway.

Alice wanted to ask if she should be ready to give a report to her father as well, but her head felt heavy. Tomorrow. Everything would look better tomorrow.

Christian easily carried her upstairs as if she weighed nothing, and deposited her on her bed at her mother's direction. Before he drew away, however, Alice felt his kiss on her brow. "Sleep well, my beautiful warrior," he whispered, and then he was gone.

Alice smiled and turned into her pillow. She was so very tired, but contentment washed over her. Christian recognized the things about her that made her stand out and would be an embarrassment, or perhaps even ruin her, if anyone found out. But those were the things that had captured his attention.

He'd truly seen the woman she was. And admired what he saw.

Warmth pooled in her chest at the thought, and then she let herself sleep, dreaming of the man who had won her heart.

CHAPTER 18

*C*hristian rolled up his shirtsleeves as he approached the Priest House where Dubois and Jasper were being held. He had so much pent-up energy flowing through him after the scene at the inn and getting Alice home that he needed to do something.

Nodding to the agent standing sentry at the door, Christian entered. The entryway was bare, lit only by two torches fastened to the wall. Walking forward, Christian found the duke sitting in a small antechamber that boasted two chairs and a table.

He looked up at Christian. "I thought I might see you tonight. How's Alice?"

"Sleeping. Exhausted." Christian sat down in the chair across from the duke. "How is the questioning going here?"

"Dubois hasn't said a word, and the doctor doesn't think he's going to live much longer. He can't seem to stop the bleeding no matter what he does." The duke rubbed a hand over his face. "Dubois is the first lieutenant to the French secret police. For him to dic on British soil . . . well, there would be repercussions in the intclligence community. Possible retaliation."

Christian looked at the locked door in front of them. Did Dubois know he was dying? "May I question him?"

"Yes." The duke raised his hand and motioned toward the door. "If nothing else, you can sit with him. Perhaps the closer he gets to taking his last breath, the more likely he'll be to tell us why he risked coming here for that list."

Christian eased his chair back and stood. The man behind that door could very well have held the lives of dozens of British agents in his hands if Alice hadn't stopped him. Rubbing his hands together at the thought, Christian stepped toward the chamber. He wanted to know why. Hadn't enough lives been given during the war? When would it stop?

Opening the door, he stepped into the darkened room that was only illuminated by a torch on the wall and a candle on a small night table. Dubois was lying on a stone slab that the priests must have used for a bed in centuries past. It didn't look comfortable, though he'd been given a pillow and a blanket. His upper torso was bare with a bandage covering his ribcage. His legs were covered by the blanket, but Christian assumed his thigh wound had been bandaged as well. From the rigid way Dubois was holding himself, he was in a great deal of pain.

"Hello, Dubois," Christian said as he advanced into the room and took a seat in the chair next to the makeshift bed.

"I'm so surprised to see you, *monsieur*. I was under the impression British agents were hiding behind the skirts of women these days." His voice was weak, but clear. Dubois turned his dark eyes on Christian. "Or have you brought the lady with you? I admit, I might answer any questions she had for me."

Christian let the words wash over him. Dubois was obviously trying to get a rise out of him by mentioning Alice. "She's already bested you once tonight. I thought to save your pride."

Dubois gave a slight chuckle before dissolving into a coughing fit. Wincing, he cleared his throat and managed to say, "The beauty does have some bite. I underestimated her. How is her wound?" He glanced shrewdly at Christian.

"Barely more than a scratch. I doubt she will even have a scar. Which is more than I can say for you." Christian *tsk*ed. "You're not looking well at all."

"Yes, your little girl playing at the spy game was lucky tonight." He leaned his head forward. "She won't last long in this business. Women never do. They have to make too many compromises that eat at their souls. Men are better at hiding in the darkness."

"Sometimes the darkness catches up with us." Christian shifted forward. "With a position such as yours, I'm surprised you came here personally to retrieve an unsubstantiated list of possible British agents. Why not send one of your men?"

"Ah, the questioning begins." Dubois coughed again. "But I find I feel like chatting with you a while longer." He winced again as he tried to turn on his side and face Christian. "Now that Napoleon has been defeated, there are many who are reaching for power. Having leverage, knowing secrets, seems to be the best way to gain that power. A list like that could give us an advantage in working behind the scenes to come to an accord with the British."

That made sense. Jockeying for position could be greatly enhanced through blackmail. "Would you have used the list for your own gain, then?"

A ghost of a smile crossed Dubois' face. "Ah, you are so much smarter than I first thought."

"That's why you came alone. You don't want anyone to know." Christian leaned back in his chair.

"That list could have led to many more secrets, you see. British intelligence agents undoubtedly have French contacts who are betraying their country. Once they have been ferreted out, I could use them to further my own aspirations." He glanced down at his legs. "But alas, nothing went as planned."

Because of Alice's bravery.

"It almost did," Christian pointed out. Dubois' face was graying at the edges, his skin the color of parchment. He didn't have much time.

"Yes. Almost." Dubois closed his eyes. "I know who you are, Major Wolverton. When I first saw you at the inn, I couldn't think of where I'd met you before. But as I lay here, I remembered. It was in Spain."

Christian furrowed his brow. "I don't recall such a meeting."

"You wouldn't. One of our patrols had captured you and brought you to our captain. I stood at the entrance of the tent to observe your questioning. I admit, your crude clothing and Spanish accent fooled all of us. A poor farmer, you said you were, your broken English so convincing. But now, seeing you dressed as a fine English gentleman, with the accent of the nobility, I must bow to your skill at deception."

Christian thought back to that night and the tent he'd been questioned in. He vaguely recalled an officer by the entrance of the tent as he'd been questioned for hours. "I can't say I'm pleased at the renewal of our acquaintance."

Dubois coughed, and when he moved his legs, blood started to seep through the blanket and drip onto the floor.

Alarmed, Christian made to stand. "I must get the doctor. You're bleeding."

Snaking out a hand to grab at his coat, Dubois stopped him. "No. Do not call the doctor. I have loosened the bandage so I may die here. Please. Allow me this privilege."

Christian was torn. He should want Dubois alive to be questioned, but looking at the man already so close to death, it seemed a mercy to grant his request. He sat down again. "I hope it wasn't something I said."

Dubois smiled, wiping away a bit of blood on his lips. "You have humor in dark situations. Your men must have appreciated that. But to answer your question, I prefer my own company. Though I have enjoyed our small chat this evening."

Christian took a breath. This was a unique situation with a dying enemy in front of him. "Do you have anything you'd like passed along? I know the French ambassador is a discreet man and would help us get any messages through if you'd like to send one."

"No, there isn't anyone." Dubois looked up at Christian. "Our game is a lonely business. If I could, I might have made different choices and found a woman to love." His hand clenched as his lifeblood steadily dripped onto the floor. "If I'm not mistaken, you have feelings for the lady at the inn. The vixen with a knife." He raised his eyebrows. "If I may be so bold, *monsieur*, don't take that lightly. A chance to love is so fleeting. Take it."

"I appreciate your advice." An image of Alice flitted through Christian's mind. Was love what he felt for her? He wanted to be with her. Needed her to be safe. He admired her skills, loyalty, and compassion. But was that love?

Dubois' breathing was becoming labored. He turned to stare at the ceiling. "If I had one warning to give, it would be to watch the actions of Fournet, the Minister of Police, very carefully. He has powerful allies and a secret network of eyes and ears that give him advantages he wouldn't otherwise have. And he wants more. Much, much more."

The last came out as a whisper. The end was near. "Consider it done." Christian took the man's hand in his own. "Rest now."

Dubois closed his eyes. "*Merci.*"

They stayed there like that until Dubois took his last breath. Christian had held the hand of a dying man before, but he'd never imagined he'd do that for a French spy. It seemed fitting somehow, from one spy to another. Standing, Christian laid Dubois' hand on his chest and drew the blanket over his face.

Walking to the door he opened it to find the duke in conversation with another agent. They turned at his entrance, and the duke's eyes met his.

"He's dead." Christian moved to the duke's side. "He loosened the bandages from his thigh. But before he died, he did say that we should watch the Minister of Police, Fournet. Apparently he doesn't have the best interests of the French people in mind, but his own power."

The duke let out a breath. "I'll send a message to London with a full report. We'll need to transport his body there as soon as possible."

"What about Jasper?" Christian asked. The energy he'd had earlier had dissipated. He wanted to put this night behind him.

"As a traitor to the Crown, he'll pay the ultimate penalty." The duke ran a hand through his hair. "Too many men died on the battlefields, men like his brother. But Jasper's need for revenge and his willingness to murder make him a menace to society."

Christian agreed. "How are the two agents that were shot?"

The duke nodded toward the agent he'd been speaking to when Christian had come in. "That's what Wetherly was just updating me on. Both men have had the bullets removed, and we're hoping to stave off any fever."

Wetherly gave Christian a short bow. "The physician is quite hopeful, but their recuperation will take time, of course."

"We'll make sure they are well taken care of," the duke promised, his gaze on Wetherly. "I know you're concerned, but we're going to do everything we can on their behalf."

"I know you take care of your own," Wetherly said. "They couldn't be in better hands."

Christian was tempted to sit down, but stayed on his feet. "So Jasper will be charged with Thomas's murder, two attempted murders of the agents, and one more if we count Pembroke, and the kidnapping of Alice?" He shook his head. "That's quite a list."

"Yes." The duke grimaced, the candlelight giving his face a dark shadow. "I've been working on a bill to provide a small annuity to those who lost a wage-earner on the battlefield. So many women are finding themselves in reduced circumstances. It seems like there is more we should do."

Christian's esteem for the duke rose at his words. "I've been thinking of how to help those coming home from the war to adjust to life in England again. Perhaps offering a club where we can talk of our experiences and feel the support of our brothers-in-arms once more."

"That is a capital idea." The duke clapped him on the shoulder. "I should be happy to support such a worthy cause."

Wetherly's grave expression broke into a smile. "I know several men who could benefit from such a club."

"Thank you. I've been hoping to start work on it as soon as this mission was over." He glanced at the room where Dubois' body lay. "Though it didn't end in the way I thought it would, at least it's done."

The duke followed his gaze. "Yes, it does. We should get some sleep. It will be a busy day tomorrow."

"I'd still like to meet with you tomorrow morning. On a separate matter." Christian raised his eyes to the duke. He wanted to ask for Alice's hand in marriage, but wasn't sure the duke would accept such a hasty request from a potential suitor. Without extenuating circumstances, society would expect a proper courtship. And if that's what was required to win Alice's hand, then that's exactly what he would do.

"Of course. I'll see you in my study at nine o'clock sharp." The duke turned to Wetherly. "I need to start the travel arrangements. If you'll accompany me to the house, I'll have a room made up for you. With all you've done tonight watching over Channing and Hutton, you've earned it."

"With all due respect, Your Grace, I'd rather return to assist the doctor in their care. They might require something in the night, and I'd like to be there for him." Wetherly bowed and worriedly eyed the duke, his mouth pinched as if he thought he might offend him.

"Commendable." The duke leaned down and grabbed his discarded cravat from the table. "Very well, then. I'll expect an update on their condition tomorrow morning."

Wetherly nodded. "Thank you, Your Grace."

The three men walked toward the door, and when Wetherly had exited, the duke turned to Christian. "I want to thank you for your service. With the war finally at an end, the role of the Falcon Group is changing. But there is still work to be done whether it's for the Falcon Group or as a nobleman with a place in Parliament. You have the option to do both, as I have done, or to choose one. Just think carefully. Especially if you're thinking of taking a wife." The duke cut him a meaningful glance, then turned and walked out without waiting for Christian's reply.

Nodding to the man still standing sentry at the door, Christian watched the duke walk back to the house. He'd successfully navigated both worlds, but at what cost? Working with Alice had opened his eyes to the value of her skills. Would she want to continue working for Falcon Group? Did he?

He strode after the duke. Whatever decision he made, he'd discuss it with Alice first. They'd made great partners on this mission, and he wanted it to stay that way— whether they were partners on a mission or in the life he hoped they'd spend together.

CHAPTER 19

$\mathcal{A}$ lice slept deeply. The sun was streaming into her room when she woke. Stretching, she turned over and saw a cup of chocolate on her night table. Sitting up, she reached for it and took a sip. It wasn't hot, but it was still warm. Pulling her feet up under her, she sipped the chocolate and thought over the events of last night. So much had happened. She had so many questions still. Hopefully she could speak to her father as soon as possible. And Christian. She smiled. Yes, she definitely wanted to speak to him this morning as well.

As she got out of bed, her stomach growled. Putting a hand on her middle, she realized she hadn't eaten since luncheon yesterday and was ravenous. Ringing for a breakfast tray, she donned her robe and looked out her window. The sky was cloudless and the birds were singing, as if they knew how happy Alice was this morning and were celebrating with her.

She turned as the maid came in with her tray. It didn't take long for Alice to finish off the eggs and kippers. With her stomach now full, she rang for Winnie to come help her dress. Once she'd been buttoned into her favorite green day dress, she sat down at her dressing table. Winnie undid her night braid and began to brush out her hair.

"What's being said belowstairs?" Alice asked, looking at Winnie in the mirror.

Winnie stopped brushing and began to coil Alice's hair. "It's been fairly quiet. Not many know of what happened, and those who do are loyal to the duke and would never gossip, my lady." Winnie swept Alice's hair into a chignon and pinned it. "I'm so glad you're home safe."

Alice smiled warmly at her maid. "Have the houseguests gone home, then? Is Lord Pembroke still here?" It made sense that her father would have him brought here to recover and be questioned.

"Yes, my lady. Everyone left after the ball last night, and I don't think any of them were the wiser that you had been kidnapped. And Lord Pembroke was brought in last night. The doctor had just summoned your father when I came up to your chamber."

Winnie put the finishing touches on the chignon. "Is there anything else?"

"No." She stood and finally asked the question she'd wanted the answer to most of all. "Have you seen Lord Wolverton this morning?"

"No, my lady." Winnie gave her a sly glance. "I can have one of the footman track him down if you needed to get a message to him."

Alice's cheeks grew warm, and she couldn't stop a smile from spreading across her face. "No, that's quite all right. I'm sure he'll turn up."

She pulled at her sleeve, attempting to cover more of the dressing over the cut on her arm. Once she was satisfied, she walked out of her chamber, deciding to go to Lord Pembroke's room. She wanted to see how he was faring and, though an unmarried lady in a gentleman's quarters pushed the bounds of propriety, if her father was present, it wouldn't be untoward.

Going to the stairs that led to the guest wing, she hoped to catch a glimpse of Christian, but he was nowhere to be seen. She pushed down her disappointment, and knocked on Lord Pembroke's door.

"Enter," her father's voice intoned.

She opened the door and was surprised to see Lord Pembroke in the receiving area of his chamber instead of his bed. He was in a nightshirt and banyan, sitting in a chair next to the fire, her father standing next to him. He must be feeling better, then.

"I'm glad to see you up and about, my lord," she said, moving into the room and smiling down at him.

Lord Pembroke made to stand, but clutched his head and sank back down. "Forgive me, my lady, but I have the devil's own ache in my head. It was those drugs I was given." He rested his elbow on the arm of the chair and rubbed his temples. "I can't apologize enough for Jasper. I want you to know I had no idea what he was up to." His hands lowered, his fingers clenching in his lap as he spoke. Alice's heart pricked with compassion.

"You've been through so much because of him," she said, taking the chair next to his and sitting down. "I'm sure you feel wretched about the whole thing."

Her father moved to the left, until he was standing directly in front of Pembroke. "How did your valet get a list like that?"

Pembroke glanced up at him, fingering his nightshirt cuff. "I wasn't allowed in the military because I'm the sole heir to the Pembroke title. But I wanted to serve my country." He shifted his gaze to Alice. "I thought if I showed I could get information, I could prove myself and gain a position in the Foreign Office." He stopped talking and hung his head, letting out a deep exhale.

"How did you get that list?" her father asked again, but softly this time.

"I know a widow whose husband had worked for the Foreign Office. He had a bundle of papers that he'd taken home and hidden. The widow found herself in reduced circumstances after he died, and when I found out about the papers, I offered to buy them. The purchase would help her with necessities and help me gain a position, I thought." He sounded weary and regretful, as if the weight of the world rested on his shoulders.

"What went wrong?" Alice asked when Pembroke paused again.

"The papers only held the man's suspicions, with names of people he thought *could* be spies. When I saw your name and your father's name, I knew the man must have been mistaken and possibly mad. Who would ever believe that someone of your rank would ever debase themselves with spying, Your Grace? And a female spy who is also a duke's daughter? Preposterous. I disregarded the rest of the man's writings and put them away in a hidden drawer in my study. But Jasper must have found the papers and believed their contents." He reached for Alice's hand. "I can't apologize enough for any damage I've caused."

Alice looked at her father. Pembroke didn't believe they were spies. It couldn't be more perfect. "It's quite all right, Lord Pembroke. No harm done," she told him as she patted his hand. "Jasper will answer for his crimes."

"Yes, he will," her father agreed. "He'll be taken to Newgate this morning. I've arranged for the transportation of him and his brother."

Pembroke touched his head and winced. "His brother was the one who clobbered me over the head, then drugged me. I don't remember anything about the carriage ride to the inn at all."

"I was quite worried about you," Alice said, leaning forward in her seat. "I'm glad to see you are recovering."

Pembroke mustered a smile that looked more like a grimace. "Once I am truly recovered, I hope we can resume our courtship, my lady."

Alice breathed deeply, hating to squelch the hope in his eyes, but knowing it had to be done. "Lord Pembroke, you do me a great honor, but I'm afraid we won't suit. I hope you'll understand."

Pembroke's face fell and his brows furrowed tightly together. "Lady Alice, I beg you to reconsider. I know things have been a bit chaotic surrounding my circumstances, but I feel like we would make a splendid match."

Alice looked at her father, hoping for a bit of help. He gave her a small shake of his head to let her know she was on her own, and turned to face the fire to give them a modicum of privacy. "I'm sorry, my lord, but my feelings are engaged elsewhere."

Pembroke slumped back in his chair with a great sigh. "It's Wolverton, isn't it?"

Alice put her hand on his forearm. "I hope we can always be friends, Lord Pembroke. I enjoyed our conversations very much."

"If you marry Wolverton, I'll be lucky to ever gaze on you again," Pembroke grumbled. "He's a very possessive sort, from what I can gather."

Alice stifled a laugh. "Yes, well, I'm an independent woman and capable of choosing my friends." She stood. "I do wish you the very best. And I'm glad you can finally clear your name."

Pembroke reached out and kissed her hand before she could move away. "Thank you for believing in me when no one else did. That meant a lot to me."

She squeezed his hand and stepped toward the doorway.

Her father turned back to Pembroke. "Let me know if you require anything else, Lord Pembroke. My physician will be made available to you, and you are welcome to stay as long as you need to."

"Thank you, Your Grace," Pembroke said, his eyes gazing into the fire. "I suppose I shall have to begin searching for a new valet."

"Yes, quite." Her father stifled a smile as he caught up to her. They walked into the hallway, and the duke closed the door behind him.

"You handled that well," he commented as they walked down the staircase. "I'm glad to hear about your feelings for Wolverton. I think he would be relieved as well, since he was in my study early this morning, asking my permission to formally court you."

Alice's stomach did a little flip. "And what was your answer?"

"That as long as you agree, I would be happy to approve a courtship." He leaned in to smile at her with a twinkle in his eye. "And I might have mentioned that with his reputation as a tracker who can find anything or anyone, I was surprised it took him this long to finally find the woman for him."

Alice stopped on the stairs and gaped at him. "You didn't!" At her father's nod, she laughed.

Her father joined in. It felt good to have something to laugh about. She wished she could have seen Christian's face at her father's comment. That thought started the peals of laughter again and she held her stomach. Breathing deeply, Alice finally recovered, until her father held up his palms.

"Well, he did agree with me," the duke said, and that started her laughing again.

Gasping, Alice went up on tiptoes to kiss her father on the cheek. "I love you, Papa."

"And I love you, too. Now I must go find your mother. She and Cook are preparing a food basket for our ride back to London. She'll be happy when Jasper and Dubois are far away from here." The duke's hand tightened on the stair railing. "So will I, actually. Dubois loosened his bandages and bled to death in the night. But Wolverton persuaded him to give us some valuable information that might help solidify the peace we've been working so hard for. And that's because of you."

"I'm glad it's over," Alice said, sorry Dubois had died, but grateful the list was safe.

"The two agents who were shot last night are expected to recover as well. This was a successful mission." Her father patted her shoulder. "You proved that you could do well in the field, not only to me, but to yourself, I'd wager. That's invaluable." He started down the stairs, but turned back again. "Oh, and not to worry if you can't find Wolf right away. I have no doubt he'll find you."

Alice laughed as she walked down the last few stairs and turned down the hallway to her room. She was going to change into her riding habit. Taking Dolly for a ride was exactly what she needed.

And maybe Christian would find her.

It didn't take long before she was on Dolly's back, riding across the park. She had a sense of déjà vu as she rode. The sun was bright, making the lake sparkle like someone had dusted it with diamonds. It was a beautiful day.

She'd just neared the path that led down to the lake when she heard hoofbeats approaching. Her heart sang, knowing exactly who it was behind her. It was like she'd developed a sixth sense whenever Christian was near. She turned in her saddle.

"I'm surprised it took you so long to find me," she said with a smile. "I'd heard you were an excellent tracker."

"You are a difficult woman to track," he said, the corners of his mouth lifting in a smile. "I count myself lucky that I thought to ask your maid your direction."

"Isn't that cheating?" she asked, with a playful tilt of her head.

"Not at all. A good tracker knows the right questions to ask and is able to anticipate his quarry's actions because he knows them so well." He drew alongside her and watched her carefully, his expression turning serious. "I hope to know you that well someday. And to have you know me." He looked at her, his eyes the color of the lake behind them. "Alice, I have to ask, are you feeling well enough for a ride?"

"I feel like a great burden has lifted." She shrugged, touching her injured arm. "The cut is much better today, thanks to your quick actions, I'm sure."

"I'm glad to hear it." Their horses stopped near the edge of the water and Christian turned to her. "Will you walk with me?"

Dipping her head in agreement, Christian dismounted and came to help her. He held her waist as she put her feet on the ground and bent to kiss her forehead. "I've thought of nothing else but our conversation and kisses last night. I've asked your father's permission to court you." He pulled back to look in her eyes. "I don't want to rush you, but what I really wanted to do was ask him for your hand in marriage."

"Were you worried he might not approve?" She nibbled on her bottom lip and tilted her head to look up at him. "Perhaps you might have to give him all the reasons why he should give his permission for our marriage." She suppressed a smile. "Perhaps we should make a list. Look at all the angles."

He arched a brow. "Are you saying there might be a list of reasons why you shouldn't marry me?" He held up a hand. "No, don't answer that. Let's just make a list of the reasons why you should." He led her to a large, flat rock, and she sat down. After watching him pace for a few minutes, she could tell he was seriously thinking this through, and her heart turned over in her chest. She loved this man. This infuriating, thorough, and quite handsome man.

He finally stopped in front of her. "First of all, we are quite uniquely suited. Our talents complement each other in the field. You're an excellent guide; I'm a talented tracker." He dipped his head in modest acknowledgment, and she smiled. "So, I would say we meet all the requirements to be brilliant partners not only in the Falcon group, but as man and wife."

Alice wanted to clap her hands, but she waited while he paced away from her and then back once more.

He finally stopped pacing and knelt in front of her. "Alice, the thing I want most to tell your father, and you, is that I would promise to shield your heart as I know you'll shield mine, whether we continue to work for the Falcon Group or not, I will protect you from enemies as I know you'll protect me. I vow to be a loyal husband and father and support you in any way I can. You complete my circle, and I don't ever want to be parted from you." He reached out and took her hands, his blue eyes pulling her in and holding her there. "I love you, Alice."

Alice sat still, unable to pull her gaze from the man in front of her. His tender touch sent shivers down her spine, but it wasn't enough. She wanted more. Pushing off the rock, she gained her feet and pulled him up with her. Standing close, she let out a sigh and let her hands rest on his chest.

She looked up at him, hoping he could see the sincerity in her eyes. "I love you, too. And I wouldn't change a thing about your list." Her hands slid around his neck and she kissed him, her lips parting as she drew him to her. How could she resist a man who had so faithfully shown her his character and how much he cared before he made those promises and opened his heart to her? She couldn't.

He slanted his lips over hers, deepening the kiss, and the sparks that were always between them ignited into a fire that she didn't want to control. He pulled back and rested his forehead against hers. "Would a short betrothal suit you?" he asked, his breaths coming fast.

"A special license, perhaps?" she suggested with a sly smile, her heart pounding and her own words breathless.

"I *am* a marquess," he said, pulling off her gloves and raising her hands between them to gently kiss her bare knuckles. "Perhaps the title can be useful after all."

She laughed, and they walked back to the horses hand in hand. The water lapped behind them, and Alice couldn't think of a more perfect day.

Christian squeezed her fingers and stopped walking just before they reached their mounts. "I'd like you to meet my father. If he were himself, he would love you and welcome you to the family. But before he passes on, I'd like you to be able to tell our children someday that you met their grandfather." His voice cracked a little, and he swallowed. "He likely won't remember, but you will."

"I'd be honored," she said, cradling his jaw. "And if we are blessed with children, they will know their grandfather through you. He will live on through you, Christian."

He tenderly kissed her, then pulled back and smiled. "There is one thing I've been meaning to talk to you about. If we're going to be partners, I'd really like to have you teach me how to get out of bindings with fancy knots." He touched her hair and tucked a stray piece behind her ear. "Your father mentioned you have a special talent for it. He said he hasn't found one yet that you can't escape."

She nodded, following Christian's lead into a lighter topic. "Yes, and you could teach me about tracking. Or any other of the skills you've cultivated." She raised her eyebrows. "I'm sure with your experience, you have some that you haven't shared with anyone else."

"I might." He bent and slowly nuzzled her neck, kissing the soft skin where it met her shoulder. "But as your teacher, I should warn you, I would demand a lot of practice."

Alice closed her eyes, sensations rushing over her skin at his ministrations, her breath coming faster. "I'm a very fast learner," she managed to get out before she pulled his face up to meet hers. "But in this instance, I don't mind practicing."

And she kissed him again.

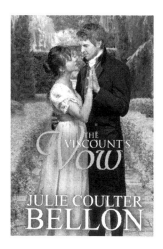

Don't miss the next book in the series!

Edward Rutledge, the newly minted Viscount Carlisle, has come back from war a changed man. The echo of the battlefield and the death of his best friend Marcus haunt him to the point that he decides to break his betrothal to Charlotte---the only woman he's ever loved.

When he's summoned home to Hartwell Manor, he comes face-to-face with her. Slowly, her strength and love make him see that he might be able to reclaim what he thought was lost. But when word reaches him that Marcus might not have died in Spain and yet lives, Edward will do anything to bring his friend home. As the mystery deepens, however, Edward is drawn into an intrigue that forces him to confront the demons that have plagued him since he returned to England. Will he have to sacrifice everything he's built with Charlotte in order to keep her safe?

Julie Coulter Bellon is an award-winning author of nearly two dozen published books. Her book The Marquess Meets His Match won a five star review from Readers' Favorite, All Fall Down won the RONE award for Best Suspense, Pocket Full of Posies won a RONE Honorable Mention for Best Suspense and The Captain was a RONE award finalist for Best Suspense. Most recently her books, The Capture and Second Look were both Whitney finalists for Best Suspense/Mystery.

Julie loves to travel and her favorite cities she's visited so far are probably Athens, Paris, Ottawa, and London. In her free time, she loves to read, write, teach, watch Hawaii Five-O, and eat Canadian chocolate. Not necessarily in that order.

If you'd like to be the first to hear about Julie's new projects and receive a free book, you can sign up to be part of her VIP group on her website www.juliebellon.com

facebook.com/AuthorJulieCoulterBellon
twitter.com/juliebellon
instagram.com/AuthorJulieCoulterBellon

Made in the USA
Middletown, DE
05 July 2021

43630929R00113